A GRIM AFFAIR

Rachel Stanley

Stanley Publications

ISBN: 978-1-8380272-1-6

For my soulmate, David Stanley.

CONTENTS

ACKNOWLEDGMENTS

There are many people who have supported me on my journey towards publishing my first novel. I'd like them to know how grateful I am for their love, support, positivity and criticism. I'd also like them to know that I did always listen. And sometimes I edited accordingly.

A huge heartfelt thanks goes to; my Mum, Margaret Eyre; my brother and his family, Daniel, Jessica, Ewan and Esme Eyre; my in-laws, Joan and Peter Stanley; and, my brother-in-law, Phil Stanley. Just because.

My husband, David Stanley, also deserves a mention having suffered more than anyone else because of my writing. It took me three whole years to write this novel and throughout that entire time he's the one who's dug me out of every single hole I wrote myself into. Bear in mind, he doesn't even like supernatural romantic thrillers!

When I thought I was done, I had an army of willing volunteers ready to savage my work. I needed it! Version two was much better than version one because these people were willing to be honest: my Mum, Deborah Gyte, Gill Hughes and Ellen Pinto-Hazell.

Extra special thanks must then go to Rhona Roberts for giving me the gift of time, without which I would never have found the space in my life to write anything at all.

And finally, three very important people in this process: Danny Cassidy, Lee Munro, and Beck Michaels. Danny helped me to understand the police processes in the U.K. ensuring a degree of accuracy, Lee completed the final proofread and Beck designed the cover for me.

My thanks to you all.

P.S. Any mistakes are all my own. I may have had help and support but the final say was all mine and sometimes I just liked it the way it was.

PROLOGUE

Sunday 22nd November 1914

An eerie silence, punctuated only by the occasional sound of distant gunfire, had fallen over the battlefield. The initial fight was over, although the campaign was far from won. Each side had retreated into their trenches, driven to find cover by the freezing cold air that had embraced northern France. The dead and the dying lay where they had fallen. No-man's-land was awash with corpses, but no-one dared tread there anymore, not even to retrieve the bodies of beloved friends and comrades. Well, almost no-one anyway.

The only one who was willing to walk across no-man's-land drifted aimlessly about, undisturbed by the macabre scene within which he found himself. He had nowhere specific to be and no-one specific that he wanted to find. He could have been anywhere on God's green earth, but he'd chosen that particular spot because he was mildly intrigued about the goings-on in the area. After all, the severity of the war was such that even animals had long since fled their nests and their burrows.

The ground was treacherous to walk upon. The field, having been used as a battlefield for many weeks, had been churned up to such an extent that great furrows had been gouged into the earth. Exploding grenades had left behind craters that could have easily doubled as graves and the soil was so heavily soaked with blood that, by rights, it should have oozed underfoot. But it didn't, not where he walked anyway. Nor did he stumble as a result of the uneven surface.

Everywhere he looked he could see the bodies of fallen soldiers. Some lay crumpled in a heap, shot and killed as they'd charged. Some lay spread-eagled on their backs, thrown by an explosion as they'd run towards the opposing army. More still lay on their sides, wounded and collapsing mid-stride before curling in on themselves to die. And with the many more that still lay dying, there was an unconscious 'copy' of himself, reaping their souls. Because that was what he did, that was his purpose. Whenever someone died, no matter who they were or how they'd lived their life, he was there to give them the Kiss of Death, to draw the energy of creation into his body. How it was possible for him to be with everyone when they perished he didn't know but, because of the copies, he was.

He had no real understanding of what the copies were. He thought of them in that way because they looked like he did. He assumed that they were created in his image because he was the only Keeper of Souls. Perhaps they were actually a part of him though, or an extension of himself maybe? He wasn't entirely sure, but he knew that they were 'of him' in one way or another because he always knew how many were active at any one time, and he saw what they saw. Also, the souls that they reaped settled within him. He didn't have any control over them though. They materialised on their own accord but, whereas he was an independent being capable of free will and thought, they were unable to do anything other than reap souls. He could come and go as he pleased. He could choose to exist anywhere in the world. They could not: they appeared, they reaped a soul, they went. They didn't (or perhaps couldn't) even speak to him. A new one just popped up for each and every person who was on the verge of death, did what was necessary and then blinked out of existence. The only time one didn't appear was when he chose to do a conscious reaping himself.

When he'd first come into being in 1027, he'd taken his responsibilities very seriously. He'd personally been there for as many of the dying as he could. He'd even attempted to grow his capabilities during Genghis Khan's campaign in the Far East. The year had been 1211 and the Mongol army had been raiding villages in northern China as part of their attack on the Jin dynasty. Refugees from the countryside had poured into the cities and the Jin ruler, who by then had been running out of options, had slaughtered many of his own people in an attempt to resolve the overcrowding. It had been the perfect opportunity for him to test his limits, to push the boundaries, to try and reap more than one soul at once. Over time, it had turned into a game he'd played. No matter what he did though, he couldn't make his conscious self be in two places at the same time. He'd always lost the game. He'd never been able to stop a soul from being reaped either, a copy always appeared.

Now, just over 700 years later, he'd long since given up worrying about the mechanics of what he did. More often than not he simply left the dumb copies to do what was necessary. If they were tools to help him reap the souls of man, he figured he may as well use them. Time had not been kind to him and he'd lost the inclination he'd once had to invest anything of himself in the dying.

While he meandered apathetically around the battlefield, as each soul was reaped by a copy, he 'saw' the life that had been lived right up until the moment that the person had died. Throughout his own life, by virtue of this talent, he'd experienced everything that it was possible to experience. On a theoretical level he knew how to speak every language ever spoken in his lifetime, he knew the rules for every game ever played in the last thousand years, and he knew the route of every mountain trail ever hiked by modern man. But he hadn't ever spoken any of those languages or played any of those games, he'd never climbed a mountain or hiked a trail. He couldn't do any of those things because he didn't exist on the mortal plane. His only experiences came from the memories of man, and while he believed he'd 'seen it all' in fact he hadn't done anything. He was cursed to live as an incorporeal being, unseen by all. He wandered freely about on Flanders Fields because he could, because neither bullets nor grenades could cause him any harm.

As time slowly passed, as twilight fell, the number of copies that lingered dwindled until eventually none were left. Imminent death was still a certainty for many, but all of those in the vicinity who were slated to die on that day had succumbed. His attention wandered. Grief and sorrow hung heavily in the air, but he couldn't sense the overwhelming emotion of others. Instead, ambivalent to the tragedy, he shifted his consciousness, choosing to exist on the other side of the world for a time.

CHAPTER 1 – BLAKE

Saturday 15th December 2018

Blake stood alone in the corner of a restaurant. He didn't lean or slouch. He wasn't bothered about a seat. He simply stood, watching and waiting. He was dressed all in black, as was his custom. Not that it mattered what he wore, Blake could have worn sunshine yellow if he'd wanted to do so and no-one would have noticed the absurdity of his outfit, no-one ever saw him until the instant of their death.

As restaurants went, the one that Blake was standing in wasn't too bad. He'd seen better, but he'd seen a whole lot worse since 1765 when the first eatery had been established. Blake had been in Paris on the day that Mr. Boulanger had thrown open his doors to the public, not because anyone had died but because where else did he have to be? For that same reason, Blake had witnessed most of the major historical events that had occurred in his lifetime.

Restaurants had come a long way in the last three centuries. Blake's choice that day was located in a converted red-brick manor house, built in 1850. It was set back from the road, deep into the woodlands giving it a secluded feel. Blake remembered the building from when it was new. In fact, he'd spent quite a bit of time there over the years. Not so much in the 1800s but later in the early 1900s when, after falling into disrepair, it had been taken over by the council and used as a military hospital. Blake had spent many hours waiting for the dying to succumb in what was now a Michelin-starred restaurant, something that the current clientele probably wouldn't appreciate.

From the outside, the manor house had retained much of its original character. At the front, a set of huge stone steps climbed up towards massive wooden doors. Bay windows protruded outwards on either side of the entry way and arched ones looked down from above. The only modern adornment was a conservatory that ran along the left-hand side of the building, giving panoramic views of the gardens.

The inside was wholly different. Inside, it was all white walls, polished floors and chrome furnishings. Immediately in front of people as they entered was a high gloss bar, to the right was a seating area and to the left, the tables. The kitchens were hidden at the back of the building.

Blake stood in the far corner of the dining space, away from the hustle and bustle of the bar and out of the walkway. He could have stood in the middle of the room if he'd chosen to do so without anyone being any the wiser, but he always preferred to stand out of the way. He stood where once there'd been a hospital bed from which he'd reaped many souls, none of which he could recall with any clarity. Blake had reaped so many souls over so many years that they'd all blended together into one long constant reaping.

Blake imagined that the restaurant was cold, not that he had any personal experience of what cold felt like but he thought he understood. He believed he'd seen enough of life's moments to have developed a sense of reality, for in the instant that a soul was reaped Blake bore witness to the life lost. He saw everything there was to see in the blink of an eye. He saw who the person had been, how they'd lived their life, what they'd experienced, who they'd loved and who they'd lost. It was nothing more than a momentary flash of insight but through those visions, through those memories, he'd experienced everything. He'd felt the breath of a mother freeze as she blew kisses to her child on a frosty morning, he'd flinched at the cold nose of a sibling mischievously rubbed against a warm cheek and more rarely, he'd gasped from the rush of cold air when two soulmates met for the first time.

Blake's attention was mostly focussed on one of the restaurant's patrons, a tall, portly gentleman seemingly in his mid-to-late forties. His interest in the man stemmed from the fact that he was as equally slated to live as he was to die.

Blake had always been able to sense imminent death. For him, it was as easy as breathing, not that he needed to breathe. He knew, without any effort, who in the room had a limited chance of survival and he knew what their associated odds were. What he couldn't do quite so easily was see how each person might die. That took concentration because, much like the Butterfly Effect, it wasn't always the immediate action that resulted in death. Rarely was it as simple as turn-left-and-get-hit-by-a-bus-or-turn-right-and-don't.

With nowhere else to be, knowing that the copies of himself would continue to reap those souls that needed reaping, Blake had paused, firstly to learn what might happen to the tall, portly gentleman and secondly to watch the actual events unfold.

The majority of those in the restaurant were safe, from Blake anyway. He couldn't sense the probability of harm, only of death. With the exception of the man that he watched, the only other people with any chance of seeing Blake in the near future was an obviously in-love young couple. They were both gently dinging against Blake's internal alarm system, but he shrugged off any concern he might have had for them. He didn't even care enough to learn what it was that might result in their untimely demise.

The focus of Blake's attention was out for a meal with a group of five others. He sat at one end of a table facing opposite a larger woman with a round, cheery-looking red face. To his left was another man who, at best, could be described as average: average height, average build, average looks.

The man that Blake watched sat mostly quiet. The woman didn't stop talking even as she ate and the average-looking man nodded along, seemingly in agreement with whatever she said. The man that Blake watched however barely said a word. He ate his meal and drank deeply from his glass, signalling for more than one refill. Having taken the time to learn his potential fates, Blake knew that at a particular moment in time he would either lift his glass for a drink or he wouldn't. In this case, that was all it took.

Blake had absolutely no interest in who the man was or who he was out with. He wasn't concerned about why he sat mostly quiet or why he drank so much. He didn't spare a thought for what that might mean and he certainly didn't care if the man lived or died. All he cared about was which of the futures would come to fruition.

As Blake watched, the man forked food from his plate into his mouth and reached for his glass. That was when the probability resolved itself and Blake turned to leave, without his soul.

CHAPTER 2 – EMMA

Thursday 7th February 2019

A sharp stabbing pain shot through my foot causing me to yank my feet under the covers and scoot away from the edge of the bed. The cat was not to be deterred though, if he couldn't drag me from the depths of my bed by attacking my feet he'd likely move onto something else. Sure enough, it wasn't long before a paw was being poked into my face. Luckily, he kept his claws to himself this time, yay me! And at least he'd chosen another part of my anatomy instead of the carpet. I would heal but the carpet wouldn't, and a new carpet wasn't in my budget.

"Cooper," I groaned, throwing back the covers and disturbing the other love of my life, Watson, who emerged from under the covers with a stretch and a yawn. "It's too early," I mumbled, even though it wasn't, before leaving them to snuggle back down, as precocious little cats are wont to do when they have successfully disturbed their people, while I shuffled off in the direction of the bathroom.

Charming, I thought to myself before embarking on an indignant internal rant about the unfairness of it all while stumbling bleary-eyed into the bathroom, which was all of two steps away from my bedroom.

I'd been having the strangest dreams recently and I felt tired and sluggish. Every time I fell asleep I saw him. I didn't know who he was, but he was the most beautiful man I'd ever seen. He was classically, and somewhat obviously, tall, dark and handsome with eyes of smouldering coal and ebony coloured hair that fell in waves around his shoulders. He was dressed almost archaically, in a long, black, elaborately embroidered jacket that fitted perfectly across his broad shoulders, was nipped in at his waist and reached down to his knees. Underneath the jacket he had on black trousers and a black shirt. Everything about him was dark and foreboding but still, my body yearned for his.

When the dreams had first started I hadn't given them much thought. Not at first anyway. I'd been out, I'd seen a hot guy, I'd then dreamt about said hot guy. All fairly normal for a twenty something living on her own. Believe me, I'd had stranger dreams. Once I'd turned slowly and somewhat torturously into a rabbit before dancing naked (well, as naked as a rabbit can be) in front of a group of jeering hamsters. Not just any old hamsters you'll note but jeering hamsters. Now that was weird!

As for my current set of dreams, they weren't exactly exciting. And they shouldn't have been disturbing either. For the first few nights Mr. Tall, Dark and Handsome (Mr. TDH) had simply stood in the corner of my bedroom. More lately, he'd got closer to me and occasionally he'd stroked my hair or my cheek, but he'd never hurt me so why did I always wake up with a start? The dreams were strange but they shouldn't have been unsettling. And they weren't, except for the fact that I'd been having roughly the same one every night for almost two months now. And I was starting to think that I was being followed, although I didn't really believe that the 'being followed' thing was connected in any way. Sometimes I wondered but mostly I was sure they were separate issues.

If the truth of the matter be told, I couldn't even be confident that I was being followed, but on more than one occasion I'd seen a dark blue sedan trailing behind me and the word 'stalker' had drifted into my consciousness. Logic had me dismissing my fears. Logic told me that it was entirely possible for me to see the same car on more than one occasion: I lived in a small village, I followed the same route to and from work, and I went to work at around about the same time every day. Logic made sense. After all, I was fairly certain that other people followed the same sort of routine as I did and consequently, I'd intersect with the same people occasionally. Logic sucked.

And why would anyone bother to follow me around anyway? I'm not exactly Miss World. Girl-next-door maybe but definitely not Miss World. Yes, I have the required height but I'm a little on the rounded side because I'm your traditional British pear. I'm an average-looking nobody with long red hair, hazel coloured eyes and a smattering of freckles across my nose. And no, I'm not looking for the sympathy vote, I'm just being realistic. I'm not worth the effort of stalking. I'm not a looker, I don't have any money and I don't know anything. I'm not rich or famous and I'm not a spy. As I said, not worth the effort.

It was a mystery that I mused over again while shampooing my hair, letting the scalding water wash away the last vestiges of sleep as the 'wide awake' shower gel did its thing and the bathroom filled with steam and the scents of citrus fruits and basil.

There was a time when being late out of bed would have filled me with a sense of urgency and I would have hurried in the shower. Recently though, because I was so tired all the time, I'd become a little tardy. Only when the water ran cold did I venture forth from the shower to get myself dressed and ready for work. By that time the mirror had totally and utterly misted over. Absently, I glanced into it while wrapping the towel around myself. I fully expected to see nothing other than my own hazy reflection covered in condensation staring back at me. Instead, a face that was not my own blinked at me in its place. I squeaked and dropped the towel to the floor. Standing there in nothing but my birthday suit, I tentatively (and I'll admit it, with trembling hands) reached out towards the mirror. Relief flooded me when my hand hit a solid surface and I released a breath that I hadn't even realised I was holding. The face did not change though. Instead, it moved as I moved.

"Deep breaths Emma, deep breaths," I counselled, studying what appeared to be my new face. It was similar to the one that I thought I'd woken up with but it made me look older than I was. Briefly, I wondered if it was possible to sleep away several years but no, Sleeping Beauty was a fairy tale. Glancing first to the left and then to right I noticed more and more differences. The face that had been superimposed onto my own was slimmer, the cheek-bones were a little more defined, and the hair was tied back in a bun whereas mine was in a towel turban. That, in and of itself, should have been a giveaway that something odd was happening and it wasn't that my face had changed overnight.

"This cannot be real," I said, shaking my head in disbelief. Slowly the face dissolved. "Great, now I'm hallucinating," I muttered at roughly the same time that I realised I was standing naked in the bathroom getting cold, a fact that galvanised me into action.

I was perhaps halfway to the veterinary centre where I worked when I noticed the dark blue sedan again. My heart rate jumped and fear curled its cold fingers around my heart giving it a brief squeeze. For some reason my motor senses woke up, even though I wasn't sure about the 'being followed' thing. It was still a possibility that I was seeing any number of dark blue sedans and assuming they were all one and the same, cars were not my thing.

It wasn't immediately behind me, there was a bottle-green mini between us, but it definitely hadn't been there when I'd left my house and I wasn't entirely sure where I'd picked it up. I shifted in my seat trying to read the number plate but I couldn't see it.

"You're being crazy," I told myself out loud, in a bid to convince myself it was true, but still I purposely missed my exit. I had no idea why and it didn't tell me anything because I was on a long straight road with no turn-offs other than the one to my work. Unsurprisingly, the dark blue sedan stayed put, as did the mini. Maybe I really was going crazy.

Eventually, I came to a crossroads and had to pull up because of a red light. Straight over would take me into a little village not dissimilar to my own but with a supermarket, which is where I'd decided to go, that being a legitimate detour on my way into work. Because of course I cared whether or not a potential stalker thought my detour was legitimate. Most people, I figured, would go left or right because there wasn't that much employment in the little village. After waiting for what felt like an eternity for the lights to change, I set off again. The dark blue sedan followed but the mini turned left. My stomach rolled and I was suddenly very glad that I hadn't bothered with any breakfast. Rather than giving in to impulse though and hightailing it straight to the local police station, I continued as if I was heading to the supermarket. After all, it was entirely possible that whoever drove the dark blue sedan worked in the village. It may have been small but it wasn't a ghost town. After a short drive, I came to a roundabout and took a left.

As I drove, I felt the muscles in my body tensing ever tighter while, in my mind, I ran through possible scenarios for the outcome of my 'adventure'. Each one was less credible than the one before. First, I made it to the supermarket with nothing untoward happening, then I was followed all the way into the carpark but again nothing untoward happened, after that I was approached by a masked man while reaching for milk. And so it went on! My car was being rammed from behind (in my imagination of course) when the supermarket finally came into view and I was able to turn off the main road. At long last, I lost my tail.

"Yep. Crazy," I confirmed to myself, but while my heart rate slowed down my stomach continued to churn. Only later did I realise that I could have easily read the dark blue sedan's number plate at any time when it had been right behind me. Idiot!

Being late into work was extremely unlike me but neither Andrew (the practice owner and our head vet) nor Rhona (our receptionist) questioned it when I entered the front door of Cedar's Veterinary Centre. He simply greeted me with a nod and she just smiled and said 'hi'. All perfectly normal but both of their none-reactions made me feel so guilty.

"I'm sorry, I'm sorry," I said, trying to navigate the double doors of the practice while also pulling a hat from my head and a scarf from around my neck. Andrew and Rhona may not have had much to say but Ellie, the only other member of the team due in that day, came rushing over full of questions. You wouldn't have thought we'd exchanged several hundred text messages since seeing each other only the day before. Between one breath and the next she launched herself at me for a hug, which of course ended up with me landing on the floor in a heap. Obviously trying to disentangle myself from my winter woollies and being knocked off balance by an overly enthusiastic petite blond did not work well for me.

Sometime later, after being helped up off the floor and presented with a cup of tea and a biscuit which, as everyone knows is the breakfast of champions, I was more or less alert and ready for the start of the day.

"Still having the dreams, huh?" Ellie asked as we checked on the overnighters, most of whom were sick and in need of care. The exception being two gorgeous young kittens. They were busy wrestling each other, seemingly to the death, as I unlatched the door of their pen.

"Come on you two," I said, ignoring Ellie for a minute as I freed them both and arbitrarily handed one over. Idly, I stroked the kitten that I'd kept, the little boy. "You know it. They're driving me crazy. I keep waking up with my heart racing and I'm sure I saw that car again this morning."

"Is that why you were late?" Concern was evident in Ellie's voice.

"Yes," I answered wearily, but not really wanting to dwell on it I added, "and because I just couldn't get out of bed this morning. I'm SO tired all the time." I sighed heavily before adding, "I never thought I'd say this but I wish Mr. TDH would just go away. I'm getting absolutely no rest."

Ellie smirked, a wicked glint in her eye, "Like that is it?" She always knew when I didn't want to talk about something and she was very adept at making light of a situation.

"God no!" I exclaimed, tapping the kitten I was holding lightly on his nose. He'd more or less replaced his sister with the whole of my hand and was happily scrabbling on it with his back feet while simultaneously gnawing at my fingers. He deserved some sort of telling off. I got growled at for my trouble but, really, who could take the growl of an eight-week-old kitten seriously?

"Come on you two," I said again to the kittens, lifting the one I was holding up to my face to talk directly to him, "it's the playpen for you both," I finished, which sounded a whole lot more dramatic than it was. The kitten hissed his reply.

"He's just there," I carried on to Ellie as we carried the kittens to the break room where Andrew had installed an eight-foot by eight-foot playpen complete with cat scratchers, climbers, tunnels and various other toys for the kittens. There was a slight whine in my voice that even I heard but I continued regardless. "He stands in the corner of the room all tall, dark and handsome and…" I faltered, "well, there."

"So, he's not standing to attention?" Ellie's voice dripped innuendo and mirth. Immediately I felt heat working its way up to my cheeks and down into my loins.

Oh, how I wish he did more than just stand there, I thought, but I was too busy blushing to say it and anyway, judging from Ellie's dirty laugh, I hadn't needed to say it out loud. Maybe she could read my mind? How cool would that be!

The day passed quickly enough with morning surgery bringing the usual array of dogs, cats and rabbits along with their owners and the afternoon passing in a blur of actual surgery. It was therefore mid-afternoon before me and Ellie found time for a coffee break together. While I boiled the kettle, she collected the kittens. They were so cute that, despite their aggressive natures, it had quickly become a habit for us to collect them for a cuddle whenever possible. Armed with tea, more biscuits and a kitten apiece, me and Ellie settled into a big comfortable armchair each.

Ellie opened the conversation, "Unless you're ready to talk about what happened this morning, tell me about Mr. TDH again."

"Honestly, I've told you about him more times than I care to mention." I hadn't had a chance to tell Ellie about my weird early morning hallucination, so she could only have been referring to the reason I'd been late in, but I ignored her reference to what had been my second fright of the day, which I still wasn't ready to re-live. I sounded exasperated, but secretly I was delighted at the chance to tell her all about Mr. TDH again. Even if the dreams were bothering me, the subject of my dreams was hot! "Don't you want to tell me all about what you got up to last night?" I asked because, let's be honest, I felt I should. Thankfully Ellie shook her head as I continued straight into a description of Mr. TDH, "Well, he's quite tall, I would guess around about six feet, and he's got the darkest hair I've ever seen. It's quite long and curls around his face. It's SO sexy. And he wears the most gorgeous jacket I've ever seen, it's…"

"No-one cares about his clothing," Ellie interrupted. "What does he look like underneath his clothes?"

"I wouldn't know," I sighed, although I'd often wondered. "I keep telling you, apart from when he strokes my hair or my cheek, all he does is stand there and he's always fully clothed."

"You could guess," Ellie muttered. "I bet he's ripped, I bet he's got a six-pack and a pert bottom." Ellie had a fertile imagination but I couldn't help myself, I let myself wonder if she was right and felt my cheeks redden for the second time that day. Ellie laughed, "You so need to get laid," she said, shaking her head.

"With who?" I objected. "All the guys I know work here. Well, except for my brother of course but ew!"

"Get yourself on a dating website then. Or you could at least relieve some tension with a spot of DIY action."

"Ellie!" I exclaimed just as Andrew walked into the room.

"What are you two gossiping about?" he asked, dropping into one of the remaining armchairs and reaching for a biscuit.

"Well…" Ellie started.

"Nothing," I cut her off. "Where's Rhona? Isn't she joining us?"

"She's just coming," Andrew answered before cramming his biscuit into his mouth so that he could steal my kitten from me.

"They're so cute, aren't they?" Ellie cooed, ruffling the tummy of the kitten that she still had on her lap. It was on its back with its paws in the air, purring away quite happily. "They'll be ready for re-homing soon," she said, somewhat sadly. We'd all fallen in love with the kittens because we'd hand-reared them from the time that they'd been gifted into the practice. They'd been found in an abandoned garage in a dreadfully weakened state, curled up by the dead body of their feral mother.

"We're keeping them." Andrew's announcement was said so matter-of-factly that he might as well have been talking about the weather. Me and Ellie both sat up straighter in our armchairs. We'd been pleading with him for weeks to keep the kittens, but he'd always shut down our pleas. "Marie won't accept two more cats into our home…"

He was right on that front. Andrew's wife (Marie) had accepted any number of strays into their home over the years and had loved them all wholeheartedly, but with the current count standing at three dogs, five cats and two rabbits she'd recently put her foot down.

"…but the practice itself could do with one or two, couldn't it?"

A very slight smile tugged at the corner of his mouth. This was classic Andrew. He'd clearly given the matter a lot of thought until he'd come up with a solution, and then he'd announced it without any preamble or fuss.

Me and Ellie both squealed. Ellie snuggled the kitten that she was still holding into her and squeezed tightly. Not too tightly obviously, she was a vet nurse after all.

"There will be ground rules," Andrew's gruff nature reasserted itself, "they'll have to stay in the break room, but we'll instal a cat flap for when they're older. And your share of the cost will be taken direct from your salaries."

"Oh, erm, sure," I answered hesitantly, delighted that we were keeping the kittens but shocked that Andrew wanted us to contribute to their upkeep. Not because I didn't agree with the principle but because it was so unlike Andrew to suggest such a thing.

"Em!" Ellie exclaimed, "Andrew's joking! Honestly, you are tired if you missed that one." She turned in her seat to face Andrew square on, "You are joking, aren't you Andrew?"

Andrew raised an eyebrow in confirmation but said nothing else.

"Oh right, doh!" I laughed at myself. *So lame Emma,* I thought, *so lame.*

"Before I forget," Andrew abruptly changed the subject, "there was a delivery for you earlier." He indicated me with a nod of his head.

"A delivery? For me?" I was already scooting myself forwards and up out of my armchair to investigate as I asked the question. "What is it?"

"Go and see," Andrew replied, reaching for another biscuit and settling further into his armchair with the kitten that he'd stolen from me. Clearly he'd said as much as he was going to say on the matter.

A huge bouquet of roses sat on one side of the reception desk. They were dark red and wrapped in layers and layers of pink and white tissue paper. The overall effect was one of bleeding cotton candy that didn't really work for me to be honest. Peeking out from among all of that tissue paper and standing just above the roses was a card which Ellie, having followed me from the break room, snatched. Naturally.

"Em's got an admirer!" she announced gleefully, I assumed more for effect than for anything else because she was well aware of my fears.

"I worked that out for myself," Andrew shouted back from the break room.

I was stunned. I'd never been sent a bouquet before.

Occasionally I'd been given a bunch of flowers, usually the petrol station variety, but no-one had ever gone to the trouble of sending me an actual bouquet. And they were two very different things, weren't they? A bunch of flowers was always nice to receive, but they didn't hold quite the same level of significance as a full-blown bouquet.

From somewhere in the distance, seemingly from miles away, I heard Rhona comment. "They're gorgeous, aren't they?" And then, as though I was looking the wrong way through a telescope, I saw her stand from where she'd been sat at the reception desk and stroke the tissue paper. An oddly tender gesture that in no way snapped me out of the trance I'd happily settled into.

I wondered who they could be from. An admirer? I didn't have any, not that I was aware of anyway. Mr. TDH? Unlikely. He was a random stranger who I'd seen but not actually met in a restaurant. Who else was there? Was I really being followed? Did I really have a stalker? Would a stalker send flowers? Surely not! That did seem a little at odds with the whole being-a-stalker thing. But the anxiety that I'd felt earlier reared its ugly head again.

Ellie chose that moment to prove my earlier suspicion, the one about her being able to read my mind. "Do you think they're from Mr. TDH?" Her stage whisper was one of the most laughable things I'd ever heard, subtle it was not! A fact made evident by Rhona's question.

"Mr. TDH?"

"Who are they from then?" Andrew's question echoed Ellie's but without the subtext. He was now standing right behind me but because I hadn't heard him approach, I jumped out of my skin. My daydream, if worry could ever be called a daydream, well and truly forgotten.

Ellie still had the card and before I could get a word in edgeways, she read aloud, "To the love of my life, I owe you everything." I imagined her bowing deeply, albeit on behalf of someone else, such was the extent of her dramatisation. She didn't, but I could picture the scene.

"Em, you didn't tell me you were seeing someone." This time Andrew sounded hurt.

"Andrew," I replied as mildly as I could despite my jumbled thoughts, "I'm not seeing anyone. When would I have time? We're here from eight until six every day."

"Cheeky! You're not here from eight until six every day," he replied.

"Of course not. It just feels like it sometimes." Sarcasm was sometimes a 'go-to' response of mine. Luckily, Andrew knew that.

"So, who delivered them?" I asked.

"Someone from Interflora," Rhona answered. Well, that was about as helpful as a chocolate teapot.

There was nothing else for it, I'd have to investigate myself. Up close the roses were beautiful, certainly no expense had been spared. Each one was exquisite, just coming into bloom with the outside petals only just opening to reveal the inner bud. They were all perfectly positioned in concentric rings to create a pleasing geometric pattern, and the stalks were hidden away amidst all of that tissue paper. I lifted them off the reception desk and breathed in their scent expecting… I don't know what I was expecting but they stank! And they were heavy.

"Why don't we put them straight in your car Em?" Andrew came to my rescue. Clearly he'd seen me falter at their weight.

"My car keys are in the break room," I answered as he took the bouquet from me.

Before anyone else could move, Ellie had skipped off towards the back of the building proclaiming, "I'll get them," and after that, it was remarkable how quickly they ended up stowed in the rear footwell of my car.

CHAPTER 3 – EMMA

Thursday 7th February 2019

"Don't forget, it's our open day on Sunday," Andrew said to Rhona, Ellie and me as we were preparing to leave for the day.

Dammit! I had so totally forgotten about the open day. What was it that I'd promised to do?

The open day was a tradition that Andrew had started to mark the anniversary of the opening of Cedar's Veterinary Centre. Originally, it had been nothing more than drinks and nibbles for the staff, but over the years it had grown into a bit of a monster. All the staff would be at the practice and our clients were invited to pop-in on a drop-in basis. Usually there was a good turnout, and we often picked up new clients as people from around and about took the opportunity to scope out the place and have a bit of a nosy. It was very important to Andrew. And I had promised to… to do what exactly? Each of us always did something for the event and actually, despite it being a bit of a monster, most of us enjoyed the day and the preparations immensely. But what had I promised to do?

Nope. I was drawing a complete and utter blank.

Ellie will know, I thought to myself as I left the building and hurried to my car. Gratefully, I sank into the driver's seat and slammed the door behind me, shutting out the cold night-time air.

The perfume of the roses enveloped me in a suffocating embrace as I settled down, and it took me all of about two seconds to decide that I didn't like them. They were nice to look at and I could appreciate their aesthetic qualities, but my nose was not happy with the smell. I did my best to ignore them but that only worked for all of about the same two seconds that it had taken me to decide I didn't like them, and then I couldn't refrain from twisting around in my seat to take a peek. They were beautiful, there was no denying that.

And despite my fears, a small part of me was thrilled. People! We're nothing if not a great big mass of swirling contradictions! A part of me couldn't help but wonder if my dreams were finally coming true. Not the dreams with Mr. TDH in them. Or the dreams where I turned into a naked rabbit. But the daydream type dreams, the ones where I fell in love with a handsome prince who romanced me to death with flowers and chocolates before sweeping me off my feet with an overly indulgent proposal. Now that I had the flowers, maybe all I had to do was wait for the chocolates and the proposal.

Another part of me — a bigger part of me — was on the verge of giving in to terror. For the past few weeks I'd had an uneasy feeling, a sense that something wasn't quite right. But logic had kept me from really believing that I was actually being followed or... stalked. I shuddered at the mere thought of the word. Logic had many arguments as to why I was being silly. I couldn't even swear on a bible that it was always the same car I saw trailing along behind me. Plus, I really was tired at the minute. While the dreams were in fact innocuous, I always woke up from them with a jolt. And then my brain kicked into gear and sleep eluded me for the rest of the night until approximately half an hour before my alarm was due to go off.

But now, after receiving such an extravagant gift from an anonymous admirer, I'd come to the conclusion that I couldn't deny it any longer. There was no other explanation, I was officially being stalked. Although why anyone would want to follow me around remained inexplicable. And why a stalker would send such a gift had me perplexed. It really didn't make any sense. I was an average-looking plain-Jane and my life was so normal that even my own mother had been known to accuse me of being boring.

Turning into my village a stray thought occurred, I could kill two birds with one stone by giving the roses to Grammy. That way I would be rid of them — nasty, stinky things that they were — and I would get to see Grammy. Win-win!

Grammy was Ellie's maternal grandmother rather than my own, but we both adored her. Between us she was our last living grandparent. Sadly, she now lived in care because she'd gotten a little forgetful. Well, she'd gotten more than a little forgetful really. The decision had had to be made when Ellie's Mum (Joanne) had realised that she was getting as pissed as a fart every day on 'just the one'. In reality, because she had dementia, she couldn't remember having one and so she was having several!

The idea of seeing Grammy brought a smile to my face and as quickly as the stray thought had occurred, the decision was made. It helped that she lived within easy striking distance.

Grammy's care home had been purpose-built to look like a modern barn conversion. The building was rendered white and set back from the road. It had originally been designed in the shape of a 'U' but, over time, a number of extensions had been added and now the neat and tidy U-shaped building more closely resembled a rabbit warren. Turning first to the left and then to the right, I greeted various members of staff and residents, finally feeling a degree of calm for the first time all day. I breathed a sigh of relief and physically felt my shoulders drop just as I walked into Grammy's room.

"Hi, Grammy! Look what I've brought you." I smiled at one of my favourite people in all the world. She was standing in the middle of her room wearing navy trousers and a burgundy skirt, at least several t-shirts (just from what I could see) and both a lightweight yellow cardigan and a chunky brown knitted one. Grammy was tiny, much like Ellie, and drowning in clothes.

"Sandy! What are you doing here? It's not my birthday, is it?" A look of confusion crossed over her face and she absently scratched at her left temple. I couldn't help but notice that her nails were getting long, but they had been neatly shaped and painted pink. In another lifetime Grammy would have been mortified, she'd never worn pink in her life. But it was kind of the staff to spend time with her.

"Grammy, it's me, Emma," I said, gently hugging her into me. It was not uncommon for Grammy to mix up people nowadays and lots of people said I looked like my Mum. "Aren't you hot?" I asked. The temperature of the care home was set to somewhere between the Sahara and the Tropics, presumably to ensure that the residents didn't need several layers of clothing to keep warm, despite how Grammy was dressed.

"Emma? Who's Emma?" Grammy asked breaking away from me. "Set those down, won't you?" she commanded. It was as though she'd only just seen the enormous bouquet that I carried.

While I had hoped that Grammy would be having a good day, I brushed aside my dismay and did as she asked. I took a step towards her vanity table, above which there was an enormous old mirror screwed to the wall. I couldn't help but look into it as I placed the roses down and for the second time that day a stranger's face looked back at me. The sense of calm that I'd found only moments ago fled.

"Not again," I muttered.

Face number two once again resembled my own but this time the thought never occurred that it was, in actual fact, a replacement of my own. There was no mistaking the fact that this was a face from the 60s. The beehive was relatively small compared with some that I'd seen in the movies but it was still impressive. The lady, whoever she was, had chosen to pin up only the top half of her hair, leaving the bottom down. The resultant pigtails, for want of a better word, curled around either side of her neck snaking towards her cleavage. And her make-up! I rarely wore any but when I did I went for the natural look. The lady in the mirror had shaded her eyelids with a bright green that accentuated her natural colouring. She'd finished her look with long black lashes that framed her face and a hot red lipstick. She was stunning. I was quite impressed with the level of detail that my unconscious had conjured up to create such a well-constructed hallucination.

"Betty?" I could see from the reflection that Grammy was also looking into the mirror, but whereas I was all kinds of freaked out, she was obviously nonplussed. Of course, she couldn't see that a stranger's face had replaced my own, it wasn't possible for two people to share the same delusion. Or was it? "Betty, you shouldn't be here," Grammy continued. She certainly seemed to be talking to face number two. "Oh, it's happening, isn't it? I never thought it would, not in my lifetime anyway. I need to warn her, I need to warn Joanne." She turned away, her once bright blue eyes clouded with uncertainty and fear.

"Grammy, what's going on?" I caught her before she could leave her room. "Why don't we have a seat?"

It took a little time to persuade Grammy that she didn't want to go and find Joanne right there and then, but eventually we were sat together on her bed.

"Grammy, did you know that person?" I asked. I didn't really believe that Grammy had seen what I'd seen, although she'd obviously seen something, and I didn't really expect her to answer me, but the question popped out before I had thought it through.

"Betty," Grammy said softly, nodding gently but not looking at me. "I watched over her for years waiting for it to happen." She stared off into space as though remembering something from long ago before suddenly grabbing my arm. "Emma! You need to be careful. If it happens, you'll be in danger. Promise me you'll be careful, promise me!"

For someone so petite, Grammy had quite the grip. "I promise Grammy. You don't need to worry about me." I patted her hand reassuringly. Her sudden reaction had scared me even though I'd known her for most of my life. Gone was the Grammy from years ago with long blonde hair and a mischievous twinkle in her eye. Gone was the Grammy who was always sneaking Ellie and me bits of candy. Equally, gone was the frail old lady with silvery-grey hair that had been cropped so short a barber could have done it. Gone was the woman I loved. In her place sat someone who displayed a level of intensity and ferocity that I'd never seen Grammy exhibit before.

Just as quickly as she'd turned, Grammy transformed again. "Harold? Harold? Where are you?"

It always broke my heart when Grammy started asking for Grandpa Harold, her husband. "He's not here," I replied as gently as I could.

"Not here? Well, where is he? I'd best go find him, his dinner's getting cold." With that Grammy struggled to her feet and shuffled off, crippled by her arthritic knees. I'd long ago learned that the kindest thing to do when she misplaced Grandpa Harold was to let her go and search for him, and so I sat and watched her leave.

"I love you Grammy," I said to the empty room sometime later, before following in her direction.

Safely back at home, there was some serious pottering that had to be done and of course, the boys wanted attention. Or rather, they wanted sweeties, teatime and out. In that order thank-you very much. And only after they'd been suitably serviced was I allowed to sort myself out, which involved changing into some fluffy pyjamas and a pair of leopard print slippers before sending a number of text messages.

I'm home. It's been a long day at work. Ellie knocked me off my feet this morning. She's such a klutz! Guess what? We're keeping the kittens! Yay! Andrew says they can stay at the practice. Xx That one was sent to my Dad. He liked to know that I was home safe and sound at the end of each day even though I was a fully grown, fully fledged adult and had been for the last few years. Sometimes I wondered if he would ever stop worrying about me! In stark comparison, my Mum tended to work on the principle that no news was good news.

I hope you don't mind, I called in on Grammy without you. I decided to give the roses to her. Something weird happened, call me when you get home? I don't think I can explain by text. Xx That one was sent to Ellie.

Oh, and what are we going to call the kittens now that we're keeping them? Jessica and Fletcher? Get it? Xx That one was also sent to Ellie even though we weren't the only ones who would have a say in the names of the kittens.

Almost immediately my phone beeped in reply.

Good news. Love Dad. He wasn't much of a texter.

Of course I don't mind. Was she okay? And weird how? I'll call you in a bit, Mum's literally just serving up dinner. Lasagne and garlic bread, mmm yummy! Xx

P.S. Yes, I get it. I am well aware of your obsession with Murder She Wrote. I prefer Thor and Loki. Thor is hot! Xx

Ellie's reference to her dinner plans made me realise that actually I was quite hungry too, but with no-one to make me lasagne and garlic bread I ended up with the rarest of treats, scrambled eggs and spaghetti, all easily done in the microwave. And then I sat down to wait for Ellie's call. Well, I did debate doing some housework for a nano-second before deciding that the sofa and I were destined to spend the evening together.

As soon as I sat down, I started to drift. I didn't even have time to turn the television on before sleep started pulling me down into the depths of unconsciousness. Within mere minutes of being asleep, the dreams started up again. I could literally see Mr. TDH standing in my lounge, three or four feet in front of where I slept on the sofa, in roughly the centre of the room. He stood unnaturally still; everyone fidgets but he didn't even seem to breathe. He looked tense, as if he was ready to take up arms, with one foot slightly in front of the other. His boots, which I realised only then were knee-high, were an oddity that immediately distracted and intrigued me. They were lost in the darkness that pooled around his feet. I could see them but all of their detailing was lost to the shadows. Lifting my gaze I noticed that his hair had curled slightly around his face and his eyes, which I'd always thought of as black, were actually the darkest shade of brown, so brown that the pupil and iris were almost indistinguishable.

"You're so beautiful," I murmured to myself.

"You can see me?" he answered, seemingly startled.

"Oh my God, leave me alone!" I yelped, lurching to my feet, instantly wide awake. My dream (and Mr. TDH along with it) dissolved immediately, but my heart continued to pound so hard in my chest that I half believed it was going to explode outwards in a gory mess until I heard a meow at the back patio door. Cooper and Watson were waiting. Cooper, ever the patient one, was sitting placidly on the back doorstep while Watson was scrambling at the door desperate to be let in. He was behaving as though he had the hounds of hell on his tail and only when he stepped into the house would he be safe.

It was just a dream Em. Nothing more, nothing less, I thought, in a valiant attempt to persuade myself that that's all it had been. Because while I knew it was just a dream, in that moment I couldn't help but wonder if it had been something else.

My house wasn't the biggest in the world, from where I'd fallen asleep I could see across both the lounge and dining-kitchen out into the garden courtesy of the back patio doors, the garden being one of the reasons I'd fallen in love with the place. It was very much a countryside garden, with borders down either side, hedgerows marking the rear boundary, a small patio area and an expanse of what pretended to be grass but was mostly moss and weeds. Never before had I approached the back door in trepidation. Tonight though, after everything that I'd experienced that day, I trembled as I reached for the catch. Taking a deep breath, I tried hard to steady my nerves as I wrenched open the door. The blast of cold air was refreshing and, between that and the two little cats that bounded into the house meowing loudly, I finally felt my heart rate slow down.

"Nut job," I muttered to myself, shaking my head to clear out the last of the crazy thoughts.

CHAPTER 4 – BLAKE

Thursday 7th February 2019

Blake stood alone, hidden in the shadows of an ageing oak tree. He stood several feet away from its trunk having no desire to stand among the roots that had risen above ground before plunging into the depths of the earth in search of water. He left no impression in the soil despite standing in the same spot for some time. He stood still with his feet shoulder-width apart and his arms hung loosely by his side, watching and waiting. Waiting for what he wasn't sure about.

He was watching a particular house, a small mid-terrace built in the late 1800s. Despite its diminished stature and relatively obscure positioning (it was halfway down a narrow street that petered out into nothing), it had a pleasing, and surprisingly long, back garden behind which meandered a small trickle of water. The current owner of the house worked tirelessly in the summer months to maintain it, considering it her own little slice of the British countryside. She'd grown clematis, herbs, hebes, lavender, buddleia and bluebells against the fences that marked the boundaries between her and her neighbours and, along the rear, she'd nurtured a traditional hedgerow. Hawthorn brambles were entwined with, and wrapped around, blackberry and crab apple plants, providing her with a secure natural edging that looked pretty while also offering up food and lodgings for those birds and rodents that dared to live so close to the two wily little hunters, Cooper and Watson, that she kept for company.

The oak tree stood some way behind the house on the far bank of the brook, but it still managed to shade a portion of the garden. Having found the fertile marshy land by the tiny waterway to its liking, it had grown upwards and outwards. Now, its vast canopy reached over 100 feet in diameter. From his vantage point beside it Blake couldn't see the whole of the house, obscured as it was by the hedgerows, but he could see enough. And he could hear. He heard the back door open. He heard her greet the two little critters that she clearly doted on, warmly and with affection but with a slight wobble in the voice. He heard the back door close again. And he distinctly heard the 'click' as it was locked, not that that mattered to him. And then the house was plunged into silence.

Blake remained standing where he was, contemplating what had just happened. For days now he'd been drawn to her. He didn't know why, it wasn't something that had ever happened to him before in his very long life but it made him feel uncomfortable. It had started as nothing more than a whisper that he could dismiss. But the whisper had gotten louder, had turned into a call, a pull even. One that he couldn't ignore. And over time the pull had got stronger. All day, every day, he felt it. And at night it was stronger still, it was as though he was being physically tugged into her house, his conscious being yanked into her bedroom from wherever he was. It had taken an iron will for him to remain standing silently in the corner for as long as he had. But recently his control had started to slip. At first, he'd only stroked her hair, telling himself that neither of them would feel it anyway because he'd never been able to interact with the physical world. But he had felt her hair. The silken, copper-coloured strands had felt like nothing he'd ever experienced before. For the first time in his entire life he'd reached out to touch something and he'd touched it. After that, he'd been unable to stop himself from stroking her cheek. He had nothing to compare the feeling to, but he believed hers was the softest cheek in all the world.

Tonight had been different though, a first. He'd felt the pull while he'd been absently watching one of the copies reap a soul in Australia. He could have personally seen to the reaping himself if he'd have wanted to do so because, let's be honest, he had nothing else to do other than reap the souls of the dying, but he hadn't been able to summon up the inclination. And then, before he'd known what was happening, he'd been standing in front her. And he was sure she'd seen him. No-one had ever seen him before, not until the moment of their death anyway.

Blake wasn't worried about the soul in Australia. He hadn't even given it a second thought, partly because he wasn't really bothered about it but partly because he knew that regardless of his conscious involvement (or lack thereof) it would still have been reaped. All souls were reaped no matter what he did or didn't do because that was his job, that was what he did. Wherever he was and whatever he was doing, he was also reaping over a hundred souls a minute. It was just how it worked. He, or in actual fact a copy of himself but he didn't distinguish between the two, was where he needed to be when he needed to be.

Blake had never understood how the copies worked. Their very existence was a mystery to him, but as he stood watching the small mid-terraced house from underneath the ageing oak tree, because of them, he was also reaping two souls in Africa, hovering over 107 people worldwide waiting for them to take their last breaths, and watching 538 more who would surely die in the next five minutes. Blake didn't know how he could do all that he could do, he just did it.

Blake continued to watch the house, lost in thought, brooding. How dare a mere mortal exert such control over him? How was it even possible? Blake had been reaping souls for almost a thousand years and not once had anything out of the ordinary happened. His time had been spent drifting through life as a spiritual entity unable to engage with the physical world.

A while later, Blake didn't notice exactly when, a dog appeared and sat by his side. Colouring aside, it looked like a German shepherd, if a German shepherd had been crossed with a werewolf that is. It was massive, much bigger than any German shepherd ever born, much bigger than any wolf ever born, only the mythical werewolf could match its size and stature. Unlike a German shepherd though, its fur was mostly black but seemingly tinged with green. Underneath the shadows cast by the oak tree it most definitely looked black but when the moonlight shone through the branches, green highlights were clearly illuminated.

"Hello Seith," Blake greeted the dog after it had been sat for a while and then he tilted his head, appearing to listen.

"No, I don't understand it," he replied, "I don't like it either. She seems to be able to control me," he paused and listened some more. "No, you know that this has never happened to me before," and lastly he added, "I'm not sure what I can do about it. It's not like I can kill her, I can only reap the souls of the dying, it's not in my gift to intervene."

CHAPTER 5 – EMMA

Saturday 9th February 2019

"He can't have been in your room Em," Ellie was saying.

"I know that," I sighed, exasperated. "I'm not saying he *was* in my room. I'm saying that, for a brief moment, I *thought* he was in my room."

We'd had this conversation, or a similar one along the same lines, repeatedly over the last two days. In fact, ever since I'd found Mr. TDH standing in my lounge. Well, not actually standing there because it had just been a dream. I had to keep reminding myself that that had to have been the case though because, while I knew that there was no other explanation, I couldn't shake the feeling that it had been something else. It had been so realistic. He'd spoken to me and I, like an idiot, had called him beautiful. Or did he speak to me after I'd called him beautiful? I'd spent the last forty-odd hours turning this one little detail over and over and well, you get the message. I simply could not remember the exact sequence of events. On the one hand, my new preoccupation made a nice change from the gnawing worry that someone was stalking me. But on the other hand, it simply added to my list of fixations. Now, not only was I tired from lack of sleep and concerned about being stalked, I was also tormenting myself about the most inconsequential detail of a dream. Oh and avoiding all reflective surfaces just in case. I hadn't looked into a mirror since seeing face number two.

"Em?" Ellie asked sharply. We were walking side by side along one of the walkways in the Trafford Centre, having decided on an afternoon out. She'd clearly said something to me that, just as clearly, I hadn't heard. "You weren't listening to me, were you?" Oops, busted! She stopped and turned to face me, hands on hips. She didn't scare me though, not much anyway. Ellie might only be five-foot-six, compared to my five-foot-ten, but she could be intimidating when she wanted to be. Mostly she was a sweet, not-so-innocent, petite blonde, but every now and again she hinted at being a not-so-sweet, not-so-innocent petite blonde.

"I'm sorry, I…" I started to say before Ellie interrupted me.

"No, don't. I get it, I really do. It's just... I'm starting to get a little bit worried about you. And before you say it…" she held up her hands to stop me from interrupting even before I could open my mouth in protest, "…I know I swore I wouldn't, but we both know that a pinky pact from twenty years ago was never going to stop me. You're my best friend. You're exhausted. You're obsessing over a guy so much so that you dream about him every night. You think you're being stalked, and now you're hallucinating faces that aren't yours when you look in the mirror."

Ellie paused for breath and I was finally able to get a word in edgeways. "What if there's something wrong with me?" I asked in a small voice, surprising us both because that hadn't been what I'd been going to say. I'd been going to berate Ellie for breaking our pinky pact, the one that we'd made when we were only thirteen years old, so not actually twenty years ago. I knew it and she knew it, but apparently neither my brain nor my mouth had been on board with the plan.

It had been right after Grandpa Harold had died that we'd made our promise to each other. Ellie's parents had nearly split up because Joanne, unable to find the words to communicate the extent of her grief, had effectively closed down. She'd shut out everyone, including Ellie's Dad (Frank) who, in sheer desperation, had threatened her with divorce when some months after the funeral he still couldn't get anything other than snarky comments out of her. After the fact, one of the things that Joanne had said was that she hadn't felt able to let go because she hadn't wanted anybody to worry. While watching quietly from the side lines as children are often forced to do in such situations, me and Ellie had come to the perfectly rational conclusion that we therefore needed to promise each other never to worry about the other one.

"We'll figure something out," Ellie replied gently. "We always do, and I'll be right there with you throughout whatever this is until it's all safely in the past." She was clearly taken aback because I hadn't said the obvious, but somehow she'd still found the right words to comfort me. "Now," she continued, abruptly changing the subject and grabbing me by the hand, pulling me into motion, "we have some serious shopping to do. You're definitely safe here. Mr. TDH cannot possibly haunt you while you're awake and walking around the Trafford Centre and, even if you are being stalked, whoever it is can't try anything with all of these people about. So, let's forget everything and just shop. Promise me you'll at least try." She gave me a stern look. Ellie was the most easy-going, good-natured, affable individual that you could ever wish to meet. And the most loyal. However, she had a column of steel running through her core and I quailed when given 'the look'.

"I promise," I said. "Lead on."

And I really did try. To a degree, I even succeeded until I saw him. Mr. TDH that is, not the stalker, assuming there was a stalker because I was back to questioning the likelihood of that.

Me and Ellie had been to almost every single shop in the Trafford Centre when it happened. I'd tried on multiple new outfits (studiously avoiding looking in any of the changing room mirrors, instead relying on Ellie's opinion alone), but had bought nothing other than a pair of heels. They were the most gorgeous things I'd ever seen. They were sling-backs, of which I was not normally a fan, but they were so beautiful. They were a dusky shade of pink with a stiletto heel and a pointed toe. They had a little scalloped pattern around the top line of the shoe and I had fallen head over heels in love with them. Of course, they were totally impractical and I had nothing that would go with them. But I'd bought them anyway.

We'd talked about everything other than my issues. We'd gossiped about all of our friends and family. We'd discussed Andrew's change of heart concerning the kittens, now called Jessica and Fletcher (or Fletch for short) because I'd won that one! We'd dissected the love lives of various social media celebrities and I was actually starting to relax. But then, there he was.

We were in a coffee shop when it happened.

"My feet are killing me," I groaned as we both slumped into the depths of an oversized sofa. It was perfectly positioned just inside the coffee shop with a view out into the Trafford Centre so that we could watch the world go by while having our 'coffee', also known as a milk chocolate and cream Frappuccino with an extra shot of chocolate syrup. Yum!

"Mine too," Ellie replied. "Let's have this and then head home. We've still got our baking to do for the open day tomorrow, haven't we?" 'This' was the most enormous slice of lemon drizzle cake ever seen in either of the two hemispheres. And we had a slice each! Luckily, we didn't have to balance them on our knees because there was a little coffee table in front of the sofa that we'd secured.

"That sounds like a plan," I answered. "What did we promise to make again?" I asked, forking the biggest piece of cake possible into my mouth.

"The usual of course, Grammy's cookies and some ginger loaf cupcakes. We said we'd make some bunting as well but Rhona told me yesterday that she's already done quite a bit, so we're off the hook for that. Have you got all the ingredients in or do we need to swing by the supermarket on the way home?"

"I've got everything in already," I said despite the mouthful of cake, and I knew I would have because when circumstances were normal I was quite the baker. My baked goods didn't always look like anything to write home about, but they always tasted pretty darn good, even if I did say so myself. I had many, many happy memories of baking with Grammy, who'd taught me and Ellie everything that she knew. It was her cookie recipe that we would make later and her ginger loaf recipe that we'd adapted into a cupcake recipe. I smiled to myself thinking about a time when we'd been five or six years old and had insisted on adding food colouring to a batch of cookies we were making. They came out of the oven a curious mottled bluey-green colour, much to our dismay. They'd tasted nice of course, but they had looked a little mouldy.

"Let me guess," Ellie said, breaking into my thoughts. "The coloured cookies?"

"Am I that obvious?" I laughed.

"A little bit. But it's a classic. I think we talk about it every year when we get ready for the open day because we always end up baking Grammy's cookies. I don't know why you asked the question to be honest, we always make the same thing for the open day, we're famous for it."

"I know, I know, I guess I really am that…" tired because of Mr. TDH is what I was going to say but, as I was answering Ellie, I looked out across the Trafford Centre and there he was. I jerked upright in my seat, the fork that I was holding sliding to the floor with a clatter. "Oh my God Ellie, it's him. He's right there."

And he was right there. Mr. TDH. Almost as though my stray thought had summoned him. He was standing right there in the Trafford Centre, in the doorway of one of the shops opposite where me and Ellie sat. He looked like he always did apart from the fact that in his hands he held a huge scythe, which he used to slash downwards at the empty air. He wore a dark scowl on his face and he was staring straight at me. His hooded eyes were narrowed into a piercing glare that seemed to penetrate my very being.

"Who Em? Who's right where?" Ellie asked, craning her neck to look where I was looking. "I don't see anyone."

"You don't see anyone?" I glanced at her before looking back at Mr. TDH, pointing towards him as though Ellie had gone mad. "You don't see him? How can you not see him, he's carrying a huge fuck-off blade for heaven's sake. He doesn't exactly blend in." As I ranted, I scrambled to my feet and attempted to step over the little coffee table in front of us. It didn't work out terribly well though and I ended up tripping, swan diving head first across the table — cutlery and crockery going flying — and face planting myself into the carpet. By the time I'd righted myself, Mr. TDH was gone and Ellie was pulling me up.

"I'm sorry, I really don't see anyone. There's no-one where you were pointing, not even a store assistant."

"Well, there isn't now. He's gone now, but he was right there. How could you not see him? Do you think I'm seeing more than just random faces in the mirror now? Or do you think I'm lying? That's it, isn't it? You think I'm lying," I continued to rant.

Ellie cut in. "I don't think you're lying." She sounded very placid, presumably in an attempt to calm me down but, if anything, her serenity fuelled the fire that was stoking my temper.

"So, I'm going crazy?" I asked. The shrill hysteria even reached my own ears but I resolutely tuned it out. "If I'm not lying, that must be it. I'm officially going completely and utterly crazy!" I paused for breath and in a quieter voice added, "He was right there, he looked straight at me. And he was carrying a scythe. Who does that?"

"Come on," Ellie urged, gathering our belongings. "It's time for home anyway."

"You're not answering me," I accused. "You do think I'm going crazy."

"Don't be daft, you're not crazy. You are, however, overtired. Come on, let's go," she finished, dragging me in the direction of her car, ignoring my continued protests.

I'd be lying if I said I didn't sulk a little bit on the way home. I sat slumped in the passenger seat of Ellie's car and stared out of the window in a moody silence while she drove us back to my place. Apparently, Ellie thought I was too tired to drive long distances at the minute, so she'd driven us to the Trafford Centre earlier that day. Apparently, Ellie also thought I was a crazy liar.

I muttered some choice phrases under my breath when we first got into the car, but Ellie completely and utterly ignored me. She was seemingly oblivious to the frosty atmosphere that I was working so hard to develop and consequently I reverted to 'having my say' in my head. While I fumed in silence, maintaining the chill, she sang along to the radio as though she had not a care in the world. Some friend she was!

I couldn't believe Ellie thought I'd been lying. Or that I was crazy. I was indignant. My blood boiled. Why would I say that Mr. TDH had been right there if he hadn't been? It made me wonder what else she thought I was lying about.

And instead of helping me when I'd made a fool of myself, falling over the coffee table, she'd hustled me out of, not just the coffee shop, but the whole of the Trafford Centre. She'd been so embarrassed by her crazy best friend — make that ex-best friend — that she'd felt the need to drag me out of the entire damn shopping centre. I'd always been there for her. I'd gone to every stupid party that she'd ever wanted to go to. I'd traded clothes with her, not many I'll grant you because Ellie is one of those petite, sporty-looking blondes with a bouncy pony tail and I am not. What suits me does not suit Ellie and, maybe more to the point, what fits me does not fit Ellie. But the fact remained I had traded some clothes with her, scarfs mostly.

She was mean and I was better off without her.

I absolutely intended on sulking for the whole of the journey home in a bid to make my point, but eventually I ran out of both new points to make to myself and new insults to hurl (albeit silently) at Ellie. It turns out that it is a bit difficult having a one-sided argument, without actually arguing, while the person you're arguing with sits next to you singing. She couldn't just sit there. No, she had to sing. The singing was what did it, it ruined my ability to sulk by breaking my concentration.

Eventually, I sighed.

"Finished sulking, have we?" Ellie asked, sweetly.

"I wasn't sulking," I retorted.

"Of course you weren't," she answered.

"I was just organising my thoughts and coming to terms with the fact that you think I'm a crazy liar."

"I don't think you're a liar and I don't think you're crazy Em," Ellie said, glancing at me briefly before turning her full attention back to the road. We were getting closer to home and so the roads were more familiar to her, but it was also getting darker and Ellie wasn't the most confident of drivers. I was normally the designated driver because I liked driving and I was good at it. "But so what if I do think you're crazy?"

Ellie carried on. "And so what if you are? I'd still love you. I'll always love you, even if it turns out you're schizophrenic or bipolar or have borderline personality disorder, not that I actually know what that last one is. Whatever's wrong with you, whatever you're going through, I'll always be there for you. Honestly though, I just think you're overtired."

"But, what if…" I started and then faltered. "What if there is something wrong with me?" I finished, asking the same question that I'd asked earlier on that day

I'd played the "what if" game quite a bit recently. What if I was crazy? Or really ill? What if my subconscious was trying to tell me something and I was missing the point? And what if someone really was stalking me? What if they wanted me dead? Although even I admitted to myself that that was an unlikely scenario. Seriously, who would want me dead? No amount of mounting terror had persuaded me that that was a possibility.

"What if," I continued, "I am seeing things? The guy in the restaurant, no-one else saw him, maybe I made him up. And the guy today. He was so real, did you really not see him?"

"I'm sorry chick, I really didn't see him. But that doesn't mean he wasn't real to you. Maybe we need to talk to someone else about all of this?"

"Maybe," I answered sadly. "If only I could get a good night's sleep, I'm sure I'd feel better."

"It certainly wouldn't hurt," Ellie concluded. "So," she changed the subject, "was I mean? Did you decide I was your ex-best friend while you ranted in perfect silence to yourself?"

"Whaaat?" I laughed, "I don't know what you're talking about."

"You forget just how well I know you," Ellie answered gravely. "And I just bet my singing drove you nuts, didn't it?" She smirked at me while manoeuvring her car into my street all in one graceful movement. Parking was very limited where I lived but luckily there was a space right outside my front door.

I laughed for real then and the argument, or whatever it was, was totally forgotten. Which was perfect timing seeing as how we had just arrived home.

"Are you staying over?" I asked, getting out of the car and retrieving my new heels from the back seat.

"Are omelettes made with eggs?" Ellie asked by way of a reply. "Of course I'm staying over, it's the night before the open day and we have baking to do. Also, it's been ages since we got the quilt down and snuggled up with Cooper and Watson on the sofa."

"We did that last week," I answered dryly, unlocking the front door and bursting into the house, Ellie hot on my heels. "Pookies," I called out to the boys. Cooper was already en-route to greet me, but Watson merely sat at the top of the stairs and yawned. He would eventually saunter down to say hello but it was always Cooper that welcomed me back home first, which was odd because Watson was the needier one of the two. Watson was the one who scrambled to be let in the house after play-time, Watson was the one who kneaded incessantly when having a snuggle, and Watson was the one who always slept curled up at my feet or under the covers with me. Maybe he sulked whenever he was left behind. Maybe he had inherited a sulky attitude from his sulky mummy.

A short while later the smell of baked goodies filled the kitchen, wafting out of the oven in heavenly waves of deliciousness each time that Ellie opened the door to check on progress. The first batch of cookies was cooling on a wire rack but the second batch was at the critical almost-but-not-quite done stage, and we were both keen on them not burning. Ellie hovered over the oven in much the same way that I imagined a mother hen would hover over her brood.

While Ellie impersonated poultry, I stood at the kitchen counter and mixed. My job at that point was to prepare the batter for the ginger loaf cupcakes. I had already sieved together the flour, the ginger and the salt, then I had melted the butter with the syrup and the sugar, and then I had beaten the eggs together with the milk. All that was left to do was to combine all the ingredients together and so I mixed. And as I mixed, I realised that I had forgotten how much I enjoyed baking, the simplicity of it and the complexity of it.

Me and Ellie worked in companionable silence not really needing to say very much. We each knew what we were doing, we'd baked together many, many times over the years. Our only remarks to each other were functional: "pass me the butter please" or "where did you put my spoon?"

I relaxed into the mechanics of baking and let my mind wander at will. Dispassionately I realised a couple of things. First of all, I really did need a good night's sleep! Maybe I was going crazy simply because I hadn't slept properly in weeks. Stranger things had happened. But perhaps more importantly, I needed to take control of my life. In all honesty, I didn't know if I was being stalked or not. All I really knew for definite was that I'd received an extravagant gift from an anonymous sender. Maybe I was being stalked, maybe I wasn't. Either way, doing nothing other than whining to Ellie about it was not helping. I needed to know so that I could relax or react.

Suddenly, and for the first time in weeks, I did relax properly. I felt the tension drain from my body. My shoulders sagged and my spine curved into a more natural s-shape. I hadn't realised that I'd been holding myself so rigid until the tension drained from my body.

"What?" Ellie asked, breaking the silence.

"What, what?" I replied.

"You. Something just happened, you decided something. I saw it."

"You didn't see me make a decision," I answered, pulling a face. "You can't see when someone decides something," I concluded, laughter bubbling up inside me for some reason.

"I can see when you decide something," Ellie answered indignantly. "Your posture changes. And it just did. You look better all of a sudden, not as grey."

"I don't look grey!" I exclaimed.

"You don't now. But you did, you've looked grey for weeks. And now you don't. You suddenly have more colour in you. What did you decide?"

I started to answer but then noticed a tendril of smoke sneaking its way out of the oven. "The cookies! They're burning," I yelped, changing the subject only because the cookies really were starting to burn.

Ellie immediately turned to the oven to rescue them. They were slightly browner than the first batch and would undoubtedly be crunchier than normal, but they weren't black. Phew!

"Well, what did you decide?" Ellie asked over her shoulder, her back to me while she transferred the cookies from the oven tray that they had baked on to a wire cooling rack so that the bottoms didn't go soggy. Nobody wanted a soggy bottom.

"That I've had enough," I answered. "That I need to know one way or the other if I'm being stalked, if I'm crazy or if I'm both!" I finished.

"At last!" Ellie replied. "And you're not crazy." She finished with the cookies and joined me where I worked. While we'd been talking, I'd mixed the different ingredients for the ginger loaf batter together into one caramel coloured bowl of goo and had started spooning it into the paper cases.

"I think we have to accept that I might be," I replied quite seriously. "If I'm going to tackle all of this, then I shouldn't delude myself. Mr. TDH is obviously not really there, as evidenced by the fact that only I can see him, ergo something is amiss. And it's not normal to see different faces in the mirror all the time. It might be that I'm hallucinating because I'm overtired but maybe there is something wrong with me. And as for Mr. Dark Blue Sedan, I need to know if it is all the same person or if I'm making connections where there aren't any."

"Okay, so what's the plan?" Ellie asked.

"Well, first and foremost, we're making cupcakes," I replied, spooning the last of the ginger loaf batter into a paper case and handing the newly filled cupcake tins to Ellie to go into the oven. "And then we're cleaning the bowl out," I continued, absentmindedly licking the spoon, "and after that, we're hitting Google for ideas."

"You forgot something," Ellie said.

"Oh, what's that?"

"The washing up."

"You and the washing up," I replied, rolling my eyes before putting the whole spoon in my mouth and focusing on the taste of the uncooked batter. There was something about raw cake mix, it was definitely better than cooked cake mix, and maybe even better than sex!

"Oi, save some of that for me," Ellie said, coming to stand beside me having put the cupcakes in the oven at the required temperature. She grabbed a spatula and scraped it around the inside of the bowl. "Mmm, heaven!" she sighed. "I have something to tell you," she added, sounding a lot more adult all of a sudden.

"Oh, do tell."

"I've already googled 'stalking' for ideas and I've been keeping a diary for you," she fell silent, presumably waiting for me to react.

I stilled. I probably looked a little on the gormless side. I'd been licking my spoon when she'd made her confession and it was left hanging from my mouth.

"Please don't be mad at me," Ellie continued reaching for her bag and pulling a notebook of sorts from it. "I've been worried about you but I didn't want to scare you, so I googled. It's what we usually do."

My brain finally kicked into gear. I took the spoon from my mouth before answering. "You've been keeping a diary. Ellie, that's brilliant!"

"You're not mad?"

"Don't be silly, why would I be mad?"

"I know you," Ellie replied. "You don't like being left out of things."

That was true actually. Being ignored, being left out, those were pet hates of mine and I didn't usually react well to either. "It's okay," I answered. "Really," I reassured because Ellie still looked unconvinced. "You're right, I do hate being left out of things, but I know you've been worried. I haven't been myself for some time now. And keeping a diary was inspired. Now we've got something to look at."

"Well, I can't take any credit for the idea. It's what they recommend doing and so I started writing down every detail that you told me. It sort of grew into a diary."

"It's brilliant!" I said again, pulling her in for a hug and taking the notebook that she offered.

I leafed through the pages of the notebook that Ellie had used for the diary. It was a relatively plain pink spiral-bound notebook, but I felt like I was holding something much more significant. Ellie had clearly done her research, the first few pages of the notebook were filled with notes on stalking: the definition of stalking, what legal acts applied, general advice given to victims of a stalker and so on. After that, each page was headed up with a new date starting from Saturday the 15th of December. On applicable dates, Ellie had then recorded everything I'd said about Mr. TDH in red pen and everything I'd said about Mr. Dark Blue Sedan in blue pen.

"It's only accurate for the last couple of weeks," Ellie replied. "You only said that you thought someone was following you in the middle of January and I didn't google stalking straight away. It's not that I didn't believe you, it's just… I guess I didn't think it was anything serious but then I started to wonder exactly what stalking was. At first, it was just idle curiosity, but the more I read the more I wondered about your situation."

"Don't worry, I'm still not sure if I'm really being stalked or if I'm just being paranoid," I reassured Ellie. "I swing both ways on the matter. I know that the fear is real, but I don't know if I have any reason to feel afraid." I paused, thinking about what I actually knew for definite, "All I do know is that I have received an unsolicited…" I used one of the words from Ellie's notes, "…bouquet of roses from persons unknown. Anyway," I continued, "this…" I wiggled the diary "…is great. I feel much better already," I concluded.

And I did feel much better. I felt like I was in control for the first time in weeks. I'd relaxed while we'd been baking earlier that evening, but now I felt energised as well. I quickly made a plan. I was going to keep adding to the diary and I was going to look for patterns. And I was going to get the number plate from the dark blue sedan so that I could decide for definite if I was being stalked. These were things

I could do for myself. If I wasn't being stalked then it would be a case of no harm no foul, but if I was being stalked then I would have evidence.

I leafed through the diary some more. "Why did you start the diary on the 15th of December? And why have you made notes on Mr. TDH as well?"

"I don't know really," Ellie answered. "I don't see how they can be linked, but it's an odd coincidence that you started talking about him and being followed at roughly the same time."

"Huh," I answered, not really knowing what else to say.

CHAPTER 6 – BLAKE

Saturday 9th February 2019

Blake was alone in a field, miles from anywhere. He was uncertain and unsure. Both feelings were new to him. He'd lived most of his very long life knowing everything he needed to know and, as a consequence, he'd become presumptuous. He'd always known what his purpose was and how to fulfil it. He'd very quickly learned that he was an incorporeal being, unable to do anything other than reap the souls of the dying. And he'd also very quickly learned that he was not a part of the physical world, he could not touch those things that belonged to it, nor could he taste anything from it, all he could do was see and hear. Even smell was denied to him. How he could do the things that he could do, why he could do the things that he could do, and why he was the way he was were all unanswered questions, but the fact that he did not have all the answers had never before made him hesitant to act. Once upon a time, in the dim and distant past, he'd suffered from bouts of anger and frustration, but he'd never been struck down by inertia before, not born out of uncertainty anyway.

"Seith," Blake spoke the word quietly, calling out to the only companion he'd ever known.

Almost immediately Seith was by his side. There were no sizzling bolts of electricity, the air didn't shimmer or turn a peculiar shade of pink or blue, the dog simply appeared and, after a fraction of a second, sat casually on its haunches, its head now level with Blake's chest.

"I am experiencing something that I have never experienced before," Blake said, his words the only indication that he knew of the dog's arrival. "It is taste."

Blake was both elated and disturbed. Earlier on his mouth had unexpectedly and suddenly filled with saliva. It had never happened before and at first he'd not known what it was, what was happening. Briefly he'd panicked — not that he had any intention of admitting that fact — until he had reviewed the hundreds and thousands of memories that he'd harvested over the years from all the souls that he'd reaped. He thought of them as his stolen memories because, although he'd had no choice in the taking of them, they weren't his memories. He now knew what had happened but not why it had happened. It was taste, specifically Blake thought it was ginger. He marvelled at the warmth that he still felt in his mouth. There was both a creaminess and a sweetness to the taste, but underpinning both was the warmth. The warmth lasted even now.

Blake had lived for a very long time but in many ways he'd not lived at all. As nothing more than a spirit he went about his business unseen by all except for those on their death-beds, and those remnants that remained behind after death. His only companion had been Seith, the dog. The dying soon passed away, torturing him with their memories of how wondrous life could be, and the remnants avoided him for reasons that he'd never been able to ascertain. Seith's presence had at least made life bearable, but neither one of them had really lived. Seith had always been content merely to exist, but Blake had not. He'd watched people living their lives, oblivious to the fact that they had been given the greatest gift of all and it rankled him. Why did they get to experience the wonders of the world when he could not? Even those who were evil and malicious were gifted free will. Even those who were poor and without monetary wealth could breathe fresh air. Blake had never been able to do any of those things. Over time it had made him bitter.

But tonight he had tasted something.

He was increasingly baffled by the strange things that were happening to him. The girl, the control that she seemed to have over him. The uncontrollable teleportation. The new sense of taste that he had experienced. He did not know what to do about any of it.

Seith whined in the depths of Blake's mind, rousing him from his deliberations. Seith had simply appeared in front of Blake one day when Blake was still quite young, sitting quietly until Blake had realised Seith was like him. At first Blake had been delighted to have a friend, he'd shared his thoughts and feelings openly, pouring out his fury, repeatedly asking for answers that Seith was unwilling (or unable) to give. In time, Blake had become petulant. Seith's acquiescence irritated him and he started to avoid the dog. He didn't want to accept the situation, he didn't want to be happy for everyone else. Indignation built up inside of him but, with no vent, it settled into an icy cold rage. Blake became so good at avoiding Seith that often decades passed without them encountering each other. But Seith still came when Blake called.

Seith whined silently once more.

"Yes Seith," Blake answered. "I think it's all connected to the girl. She saw me again today, I'm sure of it." Blake had no doubt that she'd seen him. He'd felt her calling him to her, pulling him to her again and then, before he'd been able to stop it from happening, he'd been standing in a shopping centre wielding the scythe. He'd been transported across the miles in an instant for a second time because of her. And she had reacted to him.

"I was using the weapon."

The scythe, or weapon as Blake referred to it, was a curved, wicked-looking blade that sat atop a long, stout wooden pole. Where the blade was fixed to the handle, seemingly by nothing, it was quite wide, but as it curved away from the handle it narrowed to a point. All of the blade's edges (including the one that protruded through the wood) were razor sharp. A casual observer might have said that only steel could have been shaped in such a way, but the blade pre-dated the invention of steel by some years. It was made of a metal unknown to modern man, and it had been impregnated with a strength like no other by a type of magic that made it sing when it was wielded. The magic was unable to burst forth from the blade by virtue of four innocuous looking runes that had been etched into the pole.

Blake knew nothing of the scythe's origins or of its magic. When he had encountered his first dark soul, he'd felt a compulsion unlike anything he'd ever felt before. He'd pulled the weapon from thin air and, instead of giving the Kiss of Death, he'd allowed the soul in question to rise up before slicing it in two. The soul had exploded into hundreds and thousands of inky black particles that had drifted aimlessly in the air before disappearing into nothing, at which point Blake had simply put the weapon back into the ether.

"No, it's back where it belongs," Blake said, clearly responding to a question that he alone had heard. He paused and then turned to the dog, fully acknowledging it at last. "What do I do Seith?" he asked.

The dog looked up at Blake, it had amber coloured eyes that gleamed in the shadows and sparkled with intellect. The dog cocked its head on one side and evidently spoke to Blake. Blake listened. When

Seith spoke so directly to Blake, Blake always listened because a part of him recognised that Seith was the real master, even if he never admitted it to himself.

"You're right, I'll talk to her."

CHAPTER 7 – EMMA

Saturday 9th February 2019

It was delivered while me and Ellie were snuggled together in the way that only best friends can snuggle, on the sofa cuddled up underneath a spare duvet watching a movie.

The film was a romantic comedy and had the same basic plot as every other romantic comedy ever written or filmed. Our hero meets (and falls in love with) our heroine, who is already taken. Cupid strikes and our heroine realises our hero is her one true love. Sod her original boyfriend! But alas, our hero has seemingly moved on. Our heroine departs feeling bereft but nobly believing she has done the right thing. But then, just before the credits roll, our hero reveals he has not moved on at all. They fall into each other's arms and live happily ever after.

Me and Ellie had seen our choice of movie for the evening several times over in the past, but we both still loved it. It made for easy watching on a cold dark night in the middle of winter. We had a bowl of popcorn wedged between us and a cat each on our knees. Our baked goodies had been boxed up ready for the next day's open day and we had dutifully (although in my case under duress) done the washing up.

The curtains in the lounge were closed and neither one of us saw anything or heard anyone approach the house, but part way through the film something was pushed through the letterbox.

I reached for the remote control and pressed pause, sitting up straighter on the sofa, disturbing Watson in the process.

"Did you hear that?" I asked, listening hard for any other noises.

"Yep," Ellie said. "It sounded like post."

"Post? At this time of night?" I asked.

"Yep," Ellie said again, "I wouldn't worry about it. It's probably just a new menu for your local pizza house."

"Really? Do you think?" I asked quizzically, my brow furrowed. "Post was delivered hours ago. Surely they deliver the new menus along with the post."

"Not always. If they've delivered a pizza next door, they've probably pushed a new menu through here in an attempt to drum up some business."

"I didn't hear a car though. Did you? If next door had had a pizza delivered, we would have heard a car." Not waiting for an answer, I pushed myself up off the sofa, depositing Watson on the floor as I stood. "I'll just fetch it, whatever it is." I was trying hard to believe it was nothing but something was telling me it was something. I didn't know what I thought it was but an uneasy feeling was slowly encapsulating me.

I yanked open the door between the lounge and the porch. It might not have been a big house but it did have a separate porch, which was just one of the things that I loved about it. As boring as it sounded, I loved the fact that all of my coats and my work shoes could be tidied away out of sight leaving the lounge free of clutter. That way, I didn't feel obligated to clean all that often!

Sitting there askew on the welcome mat was an expensive-looking, cream-coloured envelope with four words visible on the top surface. They were all written in block capitals: For Miss Emma Moore. Well, it was certainly meant for me then. I retrieved it and turned it over in my hands. There was nothing written on the other side, no indication as to who might have sent it. The only conclusion I could draw was that it had to have been hand-delivered.

"Well," I heard Ellie say from where she was still sat in the lounge, "is it a pizza menu?"

"Not exactly," I answered, returning to her and sitting myself down beside her with a bit of a plop. "Here," I showed her the envelope. She, like me, inspected both sides of it but unlike me she also held it up to her nose and gave it a sniff.

"Why are you smelling it?" I asked.

"I don't know, I read somewhere that if unexpected post smells of marzipan you shouldn't open it. I think this qualifies as unexpected post, don't you?"

"Does it? Smell of marzipan that is?"

"No," she answered, offering it back to me. "Are you going to open it?"

"Do you think I should?"

"I don't know Emma. I guess so. We don't know for definite that you're being stalked. Some days you're adamant you are, some days you're equally adamant you aren't. Maybe whatever's in there will give you some answers."

"Okay," I replied. I took the envelope back from her and took a deep breath. "Here goes nothing," I muttered before turning it over to tear into it.

"Wait!" Ellie interjected and I paused. "Maybe you should slit the envelope with a knife to preserve evidence. And maybe you should try not to touch whatever's inside it. You know, just in case."

"Good thinking Batman!" I said, nodding in agreement with her. "Wait there," I continued, giving her back the envelope and going to fetch a knife from the kitchen. Stalling for time, I also routed out a large, plastic, see-through freezer bag, thinking that we could put the contents of the envelope inside of it. That way we would still be able to inspect them, but we would also be able to reduce our contact with them.

Some five or ten minutes after hearing the envelope being delivered I was ready to open it. I sat with Ellie on the sofa and, taking a deep breath, I slid the knife into its corner. For some reason only known to my subconscious mind I always opened envelopes down the side, and so that was how I ripped into it. Inside was irrefutable proof that I was being stalked. Oddly enough though, I found it quite comforting. The not knowing had been killing me. The constant wondering and the flip flopping between I-was-I-wasn't had been a source of anxiety all on its own. In a strange way, knowing helped. I wasn't just overtired or imagining things. I wasn't putting two and two together and making five. There really was something going on. Knowing definitely helped.

"What is it?" Ellie asked, breaking into the silence that had fallen.

"It's a letter," I answered. "It's typed, not written. It says... no, never mind... read it yourself," I handed her the letter, the freezer bag forgotten.

Ellie read swiftly:

To the love of my life,

I owe you everything. I'm sure I'll never be able to fully repay you – I am however going to spend the rest of my life showing you just how much you mean to me.

I hope the roses were to your liking, they were a bit extravagant but I decided you were worth the extra expense of having so many.
I'll be honest, I was surprised that you didn't keep them, but it was nice of you to take them into the care home though, who do you visit there? I cannot wait to learn this (and more!) about you.
You're so selfless and caring, so warm and generous.

Forever and always xx

Ellie looked alarmed when she finished reading. "You need to tell people about this," she said. "You need to report it to the police."

"I guess," I sighed, "but not right now."

"Yes right now," Ellie argued. "I want you to ring your folks tonight."

"It's a bit late, don't you think?" I glanced at the time and noted it was only 9:37pm. Quite late, but not that late. *I must remember to note the time in my diary,* I thought to myself.

The debate, because it wasn't really an argument, didn't last all that long and Ellie won, naturally.

Ellie was often perceived as being a bit on the happy-go-lucky side. And certainly, in comparison to me, she was. People were drawn to her and everyone who's ever met her has loved her. She's the selfless caring one, not me! She's the warm and generous one, not me! She has a kind word to say about everything and everyone because she always looks on the bright side. But when she's decided on something there is no changing her mind.

Apparently, the advice given to victims of stalking was for them to tell the people around them and she wasn't going to go against the advice given for anything. My plea's fell on deaf ears and she refuted my rational arguments. Where I didn't want to worry my family, Ellie didn't care. When I concluded that nothing would happen overnight and that I could just as easily tell my folks in person the next day, Ellie didn't listen. Her argument was that seeing as how she was the one who had researched stalking and knew the advice that was given, it was her judgement that mattered and not mine. In the end I caved.

Because now I was officially a victim of stalking. The letter proved it. The letter made it clear that whoever had sent the roses had also sent the letter so, regardless of the dark blue sedan sightings, I was definitely being stalked. The letter also made it clear that Mr. Dark Blue Sedan assuming that my stalker was indeed Mr. Dark Blue Sedan, had been watching me and knew at least a little about my life. So far, I had deduced that he knew where I worked (because the bouquet of roses had been delivered to my work), he knew where I lived (because the letter had been delivered to my home, had been hand-delivered to my home in fact, presumably by Mr. Dark Blue Sedan himself) and he knew that I visited Grammy's care home (because he said as much). At least he didn't know about Grammy herself!

"Honestly, I'm fine," I said into the phone sometime later. "You don't need to come down here. Ellie is going to stay the night."

I listened to my Dad some more and then replied as evenly as I could. "Well, yes she was going to stay anyway. But we've got Cooper and Watson in already and we're all locked up tight," I paused, letting him continue with his tirade.

"I love you too Dad," I said when he paused for breath. "And I am going to tell the police, I don't know what they'll be able to do about it, but I will make an appointment and go and tell them."

I hadn't been in favour of telling my folks over the phone. I wasn't really sure how worrying them that night was going to help me in any way, but Ellie had threatened to call them herself if I didn't and that would not have gone down well for me. Ellie might have been onto something though because, listening to my Dad rant, I was quite glad I was not in the same room as him. And for a brief moment, I actually pitied my stalker if my Dad ever got his hands on him because my Dad's love for me could sometimes be a little bit suffocating. He was a doll, but he was a bear-shaped doll.

"No, I'm not going to tell Andrew until after the open day and before you ask, yes I am still going to the open day. I can't hide away for the rest of my life, can I? Okay, yes I'll see you there tomorrow."

I hit disconnect and sighed. "Why couldn't I have told them tomorrow?" I asked, despite my internal musings.

"Because we both know that you would have found a reason not to," Ellie replied.

"That's not true," I argued.

"Uh-huh, keep telling yourself that," Ellie responded. "Come on, it's time for bed," she changed the subject, standing from the sofa. The end of our movie would have to wait for another night.

Cooper and Watson were already nestled in their usual bedtime spots by the time that me and Ellie made it upstairs. Watson had taken himself off after being deposited on the floor from my lap, but I hadn't noticed when Cooper had snuck off.

Cooper was a big, black, incredibly handsome cat. But I was perhaps biased. He was the dominant one of the pair but he was scared of his own shadow. He was sprawled, because he seemed unable to curl, on the far side of my bed with his back touching the pillows. And his brother Watson, who was as different from Cooper as day is to night, in that he was a tiny little tabby with a big white ring of fur around his neck, was balled up on my side of the bed. At least he'd had the good grace to fall asleep at the bottom of the bed.

"Where am I meant to sleep?" I complained to the pair of them when I'd finished in the bathroom and kissed Ellie good night. Neither responded. Neither even bothered to twitch their ears in acknowledgement of my presence. "I bet Jessica and Fletcher would leave me some room," I continued, as if I could make them jealous. Still nothing. "I suppose I only have myself to blame," I concluded. Watson had curled himself up on a fleecy blanket that I had put on the bed specifically for the cats so, really, I did only have myself to blame for where he slept. Cooper however had spurned all such comforts because he didn't like anything new underfoot. He hadn't even liked grass when he'd first been let outside!

After completing my ablutions (I wasn't one of those girly girls who bothered with a facial cleansing wipe and night cream so by 'my ablutions' I really meant that I'd plugged my phone in to charge) I snuggled down under the covers doing my best not to disturb the boys and turned off the lights.

"Night Ellie," I called.

"Night Em. Sleep tight," Ellie replied from the back bedroom.

Within minutes of my head hitting the pillow Mr. TDH was back, but he wasn't standing in the corner of my room as he'd done in most of my previous dreams. Nor was he reaching down to gently stroke my hair or my cheek. Instead, he was stood next to the side of my bed and, despite it being fully dark, I could see that he looked royally teed off.

"It's time we talked," he announced without any preamble. No 'hello', no 'kiss-my-ass', no nothing. "I need to know who you are."

"Who I am?" I asked a little indignantly, as I scrambled to sit up in my dream. After the day I'd had, I was surprised to find that I wasn't alarmed or in any way disturbed by the fact that Mr. TDH was not only stood by the side of my bed, but was also talking to me. Until now my dreams had left me feeling disturbed and slightly 'off'. In fact, I'd always woken from them with such a start that I'd assumed if they ever progressed I'd be terrified, although I had no rationale for why I felt this way. Clearly the clarity that I'd gained earlier had given me a new perspective. "Who the hell are you?" I continued. "You're the one who keeps invading my dreams. And I've had enough of it now. I've got enough on my plate without my own dumb-ass psyche deciding that I need to dream about you every sodding night."

"You're not dreaming," Mr. TDH said, his voice quiet.

"Of course I'm dreaming," I argued. "I've been dreaming about you for months and I'm sick of it. I'm sick of being tired all the time because whenever I go to sleep I dream about you. And now I'm arguing with you but really I'm arguing with myself because you're a product of my imagination."

"I'm not a product of your imagination," Mr. TDH countered.

"Of course not, how could I be so stupid? You're right, you're not a product of my imagination because you're the image of some random guy I saw when I was out. Technically therefore, not a product of my imagination but you're the one in my mind so I'm having it."

"I'm not a product of anyone's imagination and, as I believe I've already told you, you're not dreaming," he said, and then he slapped me across my face. "See?" His level of sarcasm was on a par with my own but at least I never got violent with anyone.

The shock that I felt at being slapped was immediately followed by an odd sense of peace. For the brief moment that his hand had been against my cheek I'd felt as if all the pieces of a puzzle had instantly slotted into place. A serenity like nothing I'd ever experienced before washed over me. I lifted my own hand to my cheek and lightly touched where Mr. TDH had slapped me. The stinging was already receding, but the feel of his rough hand against my cheek was not.

"I'm not dreaming?" I asked. My earlier indignation had been replaced by bewilderment. I should have been overwhelmed by fear. A strange man was in my house, in my bedroom, and all I felt was awe. I should have been desperately planning an escape route but instead, I sat there immersed in wonder. The feeling of calm that had stolen over me when Mr. TDH's hand had made contact with my cheek remained and I felt oddly at ease.

"No. You're not exactly awake though, it's difficult to explain," Mr. TDH replied. "Do you mind?" he asked hesitantly, indicating the bed. His words sounded tentative and I got the distinct impression that courtesy was new to him, an effort even.

"Erm, yes of course, I should have offered I guess," I answered, having been reminded of my own manners. I scooted over to make some room for him to sit on the edge of the bed. The advantage of having a master bedroom that took up almost half of the available floor space was that I'd been able to fit in a king sized bed. There was plenty of space but nevertheless I drew my knees up to my body as I moved. Cooper and Watson both stayed put, and as a consequence Mr. TDH was forced to sit towards the middle of the bed rather than at its foot. Neither cat seemed disturbed by the intrusion, which was unusual. Neither of them liked new people, they were only ever really happy with Ellie and me although they tolerated my Mum, Dad and brother Scott too.

Mr. TDH sat tentatively, but with a grace and elegance that was unexpected bearing in mind his size and stature. Once seated, he slowly reached out and lightly touched my bedding, gently caressing it, almost marvelling at the texture of the cotton.

Why should you have offered? I asked in the silence of my mind, berating myself for being shamed into being respectful while Mr. TDH ran his hands across my bedding. *It's not like manners matter when someone breaks into your bedroom.*

"I didn't break in. I simply chose to be here," Mr. TDH replied, distracted still.

"I…" I spluttered. "I didn't suggest that you had. Not out loud anyway."

"No Emma. You were thinking it though. I heard." He evidently spoke without thought. And from the tone of his voice I gathered that patience was not his strong suit. He clearly believed that the answer was obvious and therefore the question was unworthy.

My annoyance was back and I decided to focus it on one specific point, one that had not gone unnoticed. "How do you know my name?" I asked from between gritted teeth.

A brief look of confusion crossed his face, "I don't know because I don't know the names of all other soul carriers." He was like a pendulum, swinging between apparently owning the world (and everything in it) and then being completely adrift within a world that he didn't seem to understand, not that I had time to concern myself with how he was feeling.

"Soul carriers? What do you mean? 'People' right? And seriously, who are you? Or should I ask, what are you? If I'm not dreaming and you're really real then I don't think I understand any of this."

"I am Blake. Surely you know this, you are the one who has been controlling me after all."

"I have not!" Annoyance switched into out-and-out fury at pace.

Blake raised his hands in mock surrender and while the gesture was appropriate, there was an awkwardness to it. Again, I got the distinct impression that the art of conversation was a new thing for him. "Let me explain who I am. My name is Blake, but that is a name I chose for myself. I am the Keeper of Souls, I am…"

"Wait!" I interrupted, absently holding up a hand to stop him. "Hang on a second, are you trying to tell me you're the Grim Reaper?" I asked, absolutely astonished.

"My correct title is the Keeper of Souls."

"The Grim Reaper. Holy fucking Christ, the Grim Reaper is sitting on my bed. The Grim Reaper is real?" I asked rhetorically. And then a new thought struck me. "Am I dying? Is that why I've been dreaming about you? Is that why I can see you?"

"No, you're not dying," Blake answered, although while his words were words of reassurance his tone was one of someone who was stating the bleeding obvious. "I don't know why you can see me. In all the years that I've walked this earth only those who were moments from death have been able to see me."

"Not dying," I repeated, giving myself some much needed comfort. And then another thought struck me. "Have you been following me? In a dark blue car? And sending me things? A bouquet of roses, a letter?" I asked suspiciously.

"No. Why would I do that? Even if I wanted to do any of those things I am incorporeal. To all but you it would seem. And the things you touch."

That explains his random fascination with my bedding then, I thought idly.

"Yes, it is marvellous," Blake replied.

"It's only bedding. And seriously, stop reading my mind!"

"To you it is only bedding because you have felt it many times before. To me it is so much more. It is soft, slightly textured but so soft." A gentle smile crossed his face. I got the impression he wasn't talking to me so much as vocalising his musings.

"Ooh-kay," I answered, not really knowing what else to say. "So, you haven't been following me around then?" I asked, just to make doubly sure that he wasn't my stalker.

"No."

"Not ever?"

"I have only ever been at your side when I've been unable to withstand your pull."

"My pull?"

"Yes."

"What pull?" I asked, my hackles rising again.

"You pull me to you all the time. I have done my utmost to resist but you are getting stronger. Twice now you have transported me to your side against my will. While I was busy I might add."

"When do I pull you to me?" I asked snarkily. "When have you been 'transported' against your will?" I added air quotations to the word 'transported' to emphasise that I was copying his use of the word. I didn't entirely understand what he was talking about.

"You did see me downstairs, did you not? And at the shopping centre."

"Oh," I sighed, suddenly taken aback. "I wasn't dreaming. You weren't a hallucination."

"No. You weren't dreaming. I wasn't a hallucination."

A new thought occurred. "I keep seeing strange faces in place of my own in the mirror. Are you doing that?" It had occurred to me that if I hadn't been hallucinating him, maybe they were real too.

"No," Blake answered and then abruptly stood and turned to leave. Again, no 'goodbye', no 'kiss-my-ass', no nothing.

"Wait," I called, forcing him to pause, wanting to yell at him for being so rude. "Would you stay?" I couldn't believe the words that were coming from my mouth. Stay! I was asking the Grim Reaper to stay. Really? What was I thinking? "It's just, it's been a really long day and..." my voice trailed off into nothing but I prayed that he would remain. Despite how frustrating he was, the sense of peace that he'd gifted me when he'd slapped me was intoxicating and I didn't want him to go.

Blake stilled, eventually inclining his head. He didn't seem overly enthusiastic about it but he did stay.

CHAPTER 8 – BLAKE

Saturday 9th February / Sunday 10th February 2019

Blake stood watching Emma sleep, lost in thought. For the first time in his life he'd had a conversation with someone. He'd been seen by someone, acknowledged by someone. He'd been in the same place as others before but there'd always been a disconnect because he'd always existed on a different plane. This time he'd actually sat and talked with someone, and he'd felt the bed underneath him. He'd felt the duvet cover as well. He'd even felt his own breathing. It was all he'd ever wanted but, instead of the elation that he'd anticipated, he'd felt threatened and vulnerable. He found himself retreating further and further into the shadows, giving himself the illusion of being alone once more.

For many years, many tens of years, Blake had searched for someone who could see him, for anyone that he could talk to. He'd searched the four corners of the earth. He'd spent time with many but he'd focussed his attention on a few, watching them from the moment that they were born all the way through to their deaths, standing beside them on their birthdays, when they graduated or were at interviews, when they got married and when they had children of their own. He'd celebrated with them and he'd commiserated with them. He'd mourned their deaths when they'd died, but never once had he seen himself in their memories upon reaping their souls. Eventually he'd given up. He'd lost hope and accepted that there was no-one else like him, there was no-one else that he could bond with. His interest in mankind had waned and although he'd still watched, forced into a life of voyeurism, his curiosity in individuals had dimmed.

But then he'd felt Emma calling to him. It had been faint at first, nothing more than a murmur, very easily ignored. Until it wasn't. He stood and watched her for many nights before reaching out and stroking her hair, believing it wouldn't matter, he wouldn't be able to feel her and she wouldn't be able to feel him. The delight he'd felt when he'd actually touched her had been both overwhelming and frightening. It had ignited a little spark of hope in him, but it had also scared him. Blake had never before had anything to fear, after all, what could possibly harm him, the Keeper of Souls? His life had been monotonous and dull, there had never even been the need for mild apprehension on behalf of others, because one of the things that he knew for a fact was that all were born to die. However, Emma was an anomaly, the first he'd ever encountered. He wasn't sure who or what she was. He had so many unanswered questions. Who was she? How was she able to control him? What did she want from him?

Blake had no answers though and neither, it seemed, did she.

Blake was used to unanswered questions and had long since accepted them. His whole life was a mystery. How he'd come to be was an unknown. How he was able to reap souls was another. He didn't even have any control over his 'abilities', all souls were reaped and he felt each and every one of them regardless of whether or not he wanted the job. He'd tried not sensing death. It was impossible. He could always tell who had death in their immediate future and what the likelihood of them dying was. He'd tried not reaping a soul. It simply didn't work. He'd tried not witnessing the life that had just ended. The best he'd ever been able to do was to tune out the endlessness of other people's lives.

But now Blake wanted answers. He wanted to know who she was, how he could hear her thoughts, why he could touch what she was touching, and why he was so drawn to her.

Blake silently inched further and further away from Emma until he was certain that she was asleep. When her breathing became even and tempered, when the only disturbance was the snoring of two contented little cats, Blake shifted his consciousness away and left her in peace so that he could be alone once more to consider what little he had learned.

CHAPTER 9 – EMMA

Sunday 10th February 2019

It was evident as soon as we turned into the carpark at Cedar's Veterinary Centre that me and Ellie weren't the first to arrive for the open day. And it wasn't just the cars that were parked up either, I spotted my Dad hovering in the entryway of the building almost immediately and he was outside even before I was all the way into the carpark, let alone actually parked.

Doing my best to ignore the mother hen that was my father, I nosed my car into a space next to his silver coloured Skoda, loved by both of my parents because it had a big boot. Of all the things to love in a car! The green Land Rover that was parked up was Andrew's, so he and Marie were obviously present and correct as well. And the matching blue Qashqais that also frequented the carpark belonged to two of the newer vets, Matthew and Charlotte. They'd been hired at the same time about three months previously.

My own car was a bright yellow Juke. Generally, I couldn't tell one car from any other but I'd fallen for the unconventional look of the Juke because it was so distinctive. In sunshine yellow it was perfect. Although perhaps not ideal when you're being stalked, it's difficult to fly under the radar when you drive a car that stands out like a sore thumb. But I loved it in a way that I'd never thought possible, it was only a car after all.

Because I loved my car so much, I most definitely did not appreciate my Dad yanking the driver door open with much more force than was absolutely necessary even before I'd managed to bring the car to a complete and utter stop. I glared at Ellie — this being all her fault of course — as I was manhandled out of the car. Ellie simply smiled sweetly while she unbuckled herself at a slower pace than I was forced to.

"Hi Dad," I managed to squeak before I was pulled from the car and into his arms. "Mind the door," I chastised, although my words were mostly lost in his coat. The older grown-up-me was mortified at his behaviour but the stuck-at-around-about-aged-seven-me, who loved dressing up in princess gowns and who giggled hilariously at poop jokes, was delighted. Without thinking, I snuggled briefly into his arms before coming quickly to my senses. If I gave an inch, he'd take a mile. A snuggle was one thing but I had no intention of moving back in with my folks. And believe me, I knew it was coming.

"I've been so worried about you," my Dad said over my head, while the grown-up-me took over and tried to pull away from his bear hug. All of my height and my weight were directly attributable to my Dad though. Where I was tall and curvy, he was simply huge. Pulling away from his grip was no mean feat.

"Dad, you're suffocating me," I said, guilting him into releasing his hold so that I could finally pull free.

"I've been so worried about you," he said again. "Anything could have happened to you. I've hardly slept a wink all night long."

"He slept fine," I heard my Mum say in her driest no-nonsense voice. Turning, I saw her coming up behind Ellie, who was now out of the car.

"Hi Mum," I said, smiling at her. She was the more pragmatic of my parents even though it was from her that I got my colouring. In direct contravention of the law that stated all redheads had to have a temper, my Mum never even raised her voice and generally buried her emotions deep inside her, so while I was sure she would be worried about 'the situation', she would be more focused on finding a solution. My Dad, however, wore his heart of his sleeve. Luckily I had mostly my Mum's temperament. I had my Dad's looks (apart from the red hair, hazel coloured eyes and freckles) but my Mum's character. That isn't to say that I didn't experience strong emotions, as evidenced by the fear that had taken hold recently, it was just that I tended not to show them to the wider world. There was a reason that I'd only told Ellie everything that had been happening to me. People who didn't know me might understandably accuse me of being indifferent to most things.

Turning back to my Dad and taking hold of his arm I said, "Honestly Dad, I'm fine, and need I remind you that we're at my workplace. It's Andrew's day today, okay?"

He snuffled a little bit but in the end agreed. "Okay... yes, okay. Let's unload the car and get busy setting up then, shall we?"

"Dad, you haven't told anyone else, have you?" I asked sternly before letting him go.

"No, he hasn't," my Mum answered for him. "But after the open day we do need to talk and we do need to decide what we're going to do."

Inwardly I cursed. I sensed that at the very least my life was about to become very busy and my free time very limited. Outwardly I mumbled my agreement. It wasn't an argument that I wanted to have in the carpark of Cedar's Veterinary Centre, especially not on the open day.

"So, did you make the usual?" my Mum carried on, seamlessly switching subjects.

"Of course we did Sandra," Ellie answered. "There are two boxes of cookies and 36 ginger loaf cupcakes just waiting to be eaten in the boot of Em's car. We might have eaten one or two of the cookies though, just to make sure they were edible," she finished, totally sincere.

"Only one or two?" my Mum asked, raising her eyebrows in disbelief. "I don't believe that for a second. I bet you had at least three, if not four each and I bet you started on them when they were still warm from the oven, didn't you?"

We all laughed, the tension draining away.

"Load me up then," my Dad interjected and so because it would have been rude not to I did, giving him the two boxes of cookies from the boot of my car, leaving a cupcake tin each for me, Mum and Ellie.

"Inside looks fab already," my Mum continued. "The bunting that Rhona's made looks superb and you should see the centrepieces. Charlotte made those apparently."

"Charlotte made what?" I asked, having not really been paying attention, unloading the boot instead.

"Centrepieces for the tables," my Mum replied. "Anyway, Andrew and Marie must have been here for a while already because the reception area has been totally transformed. The chairs have been put away, the tables have been set up, the bunting's been hung, and they're already on with getting out the food."

"Is Rhona here already then?" I asked, pulling the boot shut with a slam. Mum's reference to the bunting that she'd made reminded me that I hadn't seen her car when I'd pulled up.

"Yes, she's here. Her, Andrew and Marie, and Matthew and Charlotte. I think Charlotte brought Rhona," my Mum answered, an edge creeping into her voice when she mentioned Charlotte again. "I'm still not sure what I think about that one though," she continued lowering her voice to confide in me and Ellie, my Dad already off in the direction of inside, "although I can't deny that she makes stunning centrepieces."

"Why centre…" I started to ask, but Ellie stole my conversational thread.

"Really?" She remarked as the three of us started to make our way across the carpark at a more leisurely pace than my Dad. "She seems alright to me, quite quiet but she's a good vet. She's great with the animals."

"Mmm, you always see the best in people though Ellie," my Mum replied. "Me and Emma, we're more suspicious, aren't we Emma?"

"I wouldn't say suspicious Mum. I'd say cautious. Charlotte is…" I paused, searching for the right word because I hadn't warmed to her either, "...different I guess. But Matthew's fitted straight in. He's an absolute charmer. All the older clients love him."

"You mean *all* the clients love him," Ellie corrected me stressing the word 'all'. She was right as well, everyone did love Matthew. He was easy-going, good-natured and a looker. He was tall and incredibly fit with an unruly mop of sandy blonde hair and piercing blue eyes. He looked like he'd stepped straight out of the pages of a glamour magazine. Or, more likely, a surfing magazine.

"You like him!" my Mum exclaimed.

"Not like that, I don't," Ellie denied shaking her head, and because we'd had this conversation many times over (about both Matthew and Charlotte) I knew that she was telling the truth. We both agreed that while Matthew was a lovely guy, he wasn't for either of us. And she did like Charlotte but I was uncertain.

"Are you sure?" my Mum asked.

"Absolutely! Too blonde for me," Ellie concluded firmly.

"What about you Emma?"

"No Mum," I answered, picking up the pace and stepping forward to open the practice door, not in any way wanting to be a part of a conversation with my mother about my love interests.

Entering the practice was like being transported into another world. As I stepped through the double doors I briefly wondered if I'd found a portal into Narnia. The reception area had been totally transformed and looked fantastic. All of the chairs had been put away, along with the most obvious of the veterinary paraphernalia, and three trestle tables had been placed in an L-shape around the edge of the room. Each table had been covered in white linen and had been laid with a different centrepiece, around which all the food was being laid based on the fact that some of it was out already. The centrepieces were stunning. They were a mix of flowers and candles with different colours and textures blending perfectly together, so that while each piece was unique they all fitted together.

"Wow, it looks amazing in here," I exclaimed from the doorway. "I've never seen our reception area look so good."

"It's all down to Rhona and Charlotte," Marie answered, beaming from behind the counter where she stood with Andrew. Rhona was in the centre of the room but hurried towards us as we entered. My Dad, Matthew and Charlotte were nowhere to be seen, no doubt in the back.

"It was Charlotte really," Rhona countered, taking the cupcake tin I carried. "I made the bunting but the centrepieces are all her doing. And they make such a difference. They're what gives the place that wow factor." She was right but the bunting looked great too. It was hung along the front edge of each table and around the reception desk.

"I didn't know she was so creative," I said. "And I didn't know that she was planning on making centrepieces for the tables."

"She wanted it to be a surprise for everyone," Rhona answered. "A thank-you for welcoming her into the practice I think. I only knew about them because she wanted the bunting to be done in complementary colours. Did you know that her family owns a florist?" she finished.

"No, no I didn't," I answered, truthfully wondering what else she was hiding because I'd always thought there was something off about Charlotte. My Mum's sense of uncertainty towards her perfectly mirrored my own, but I couldn't find anything specific to dislike. There was just something about her, something that I couldn't quite put my finger on but that always set me on edge. Ellie was right, Charlotte was a good vet. In fact, she was great with the animals. If Cooper or Watson needed treatment I would have no qualms about her doing whatever she needed to do. But I always felt as though she was... on her guard with people, like she was playing a role and while she knew her lines, she didn't quite understand the meaning of them. It kept me from really trusting her even though Ellie liked her. But, there were things that needed to be done so I parked my train of thinking into the station and got busy.

Later, when the open day was in full swing, I returned to the worry bead that was Charlotte, covertly watching her to see if I could ascertain what it was that I didn't like about her. She was quite petite and a little bit dumpy looking with long, dark blonde hair and a ruddy-looking face. She wasn't unattractive but she wouldn't win any beauty contests either, not that I would mind you. As I stared at her I suddenly realised that she drove a dark blue sedan, just like whoever it was that was following me. I got quite excited for a minute thinking that perhaps I'd solved the mystery until I remembered that Matthew and Charlotte had matching cars and he didn't give me the willies. That line of thinking made me realise that, in all the time that I'd been wondering if I was being stalked, I'd never once thought of the person as being someone I knew. However, because I didn't really know anything about him (or her for that matter), I wasn't able to rule anyone out. Except Ellie. And my parents. I mean, seriously, why would they stalk me?

No, I thought looking around the room. *It's definitely not anyone here,* I concluded. Almost everyone I knew and loved was at the open day: my Mum and Dad, my brother Scott, Ellie, Ellie's parents, Andrew and Marie, Rhona, the rest of the staff, clients that I'd known for many years. Even Matthew and Charlotte, who were new to the group. It couldn't be any of them. I lived my life with these people.

Looking at everyone made me feel safe and protected even though I now knew, and couldn't deny, that I was being stalked. I even felt refreshed, having slept soundly for the first night in weeks. The sense of calm that had come over me when I'd read the letter the night before had stayed put. Knowing really had helped. And meeting Blake (also known as the Grim Reaper!) had left me feeling oddly reassured. I didn't really know how to explain it, even to myself, but his presence had been like a soothing balm. Assuming I had actually met the Grim Reaper. In the cold light of day I was starting to doubt myself, so much so that I hadn't even told Ellie the gory details, only that I'd dreamed about Mr. TDH again but that actually I did feel okay about everything.

"I really must do something about all of this," I muttered to myself.

"What was that, dear?" An elderly lady asked, startling me.

"Mrs. P!" I squealed. "You made me jump." Mrs. Porter was one of my favourite clients. She rescued anything furry and was always at the practice for one reason or another. We even joked with her that if she spent any more time at the practice, we'd have to move her bed in.

"You were lost in thought dearie," Mrs. P answered rubbing my arm gently with affection. "I'm not surprised I made you jump."

I smiled warmly at her. She was such a sweet old thing. "How are you? And how is Angel?" Angel was her latest rescue, an enormous

Rottweiler that looked like he should have been named anything but Angel. The irony was that he was an absolute softie and as daft as a brush.

"Oh! He's perfect," Mrs. Porter enthused. "He's so well behaved, just desperate for cuddles." She leaned in closer to me and added quietly, "I hate that he was abandoned because he was 'too big'." Angel was indeed a big dog but no-one really knew why he'd been abandoned. He'd been found tied to the gates of a local rescue centre one night. At least his family had done that much for him. The prevailing theory was that someone had bought him as a puppy not realising how big he'd grow, how much he'd eat or how much he'd need to be walked.

"Me too," I answered sadly. It infuriated me how some people treated their animals. "But it all worked out in the end because now he has you," I finished in a lighter tone of voice.

"He certainly does. Now, what about you dearie? How are you? And did you finally persuade Mr. Andrew to keep the kittens?" Mrs. Porter always referred to Andrew as Mr. Andrew, even though he'd repeatedly told her there was no need for such formality.

I laughed. "We did actually, they're called Jessica and Fletcher now. They're going to stay here at the practice. You'll have to come and meet them with me," I offered.

"That would be lovely my dear. Just let me finish my cake first. And while I do, you can tell me all about what you've been up to recently. Any handsome young men on the scene?" She raised an eyebrow suggestively.

"Mrs. P!" I exclaimed, my cheeks reddening with embarrassment.

"What? I was young once too you know. Eee, some of the stories I could tell you!" She showed not even the slightest trace of self-consciousness.

Mrs. Porter and I chatted some more although not about any 'handsome young men', until we were interrupted by a tall, portly gentleman.

"E-excuse me," he said. "I read somewhere that I could ask for a tour of the f-facilities. It's just, I-erm, well, I'm getting a cat and I'll need a vet," he concluded by way of an explanation.

"Oh, sure," I answered. "Let me just find Andrew for you." I scanned the room, which was packed, but couldn't see him anywhere.

"Can't you just g-give me the tour?" he asked. He was so softly spoken that, between that and the very slight stutter, I found myself leaning in ever so slightly to catch what he was saying.

"Oh, erm…" I deliberated. Andrew liked to give the tours but only because he thought it was his duty. We all knew he'd rather stick sharp pins in his eyes than deal with real live people. He much preferred the animals!

I looked at Mrs. Porter and was about to apologise (because she wouldn't get to meet Jessica and Fletcher) when she said, "It's okay dearie, go and do what you must. It's time I got off home anyway." She patted me on my arm and then, speaking to the gentleman who had interrupted us, she added, "You won't find a better vet in all the land," before turning to leave.

"Thanks Mrs. P," I smiled warmly at her. "Give Angel a kiss on the nose from me, won't you? Okay," I continued, refocusing my attention onto our potential new client as Mrs. Porter threaded her way through the crowd towards the door, "well, I'm Emma, one of the nurses here."

"I-It's alright, I know who you are," he replied.

A spike of terror shot through me and I faltered. I'd never met this man before, how could he possibly know who I was?

"I…" I started to say before I froze. I was obviously stood face-to-face with my stalker, it was the only explanation I could come up with. I was paralysed with fear, the room was filled with people that I knew and loved but I couldn't find it in me to open my mouth and call someone over. What if I triggered a panic? What if the lovely Mrs. Porter was crushed to death in a mass stampede? I couldn't cry foul and be the cause of that. Time stood still but hours passed.

"I-If I may, your picture is up on the wall." Evidently my distress had been written all over my face.

Relief washed over me and I laughed. Talk about jumping to conclusions and over-exaggerating! Obviously I wasn't quite as cool as the proverbial cucumber. "I'm so sorry. For a second there I thought... well, I don't know what I thought." I had forgotten that all of our pictures were on the wall. One of Marie's ideas for brightening up the reception area. She wanted our clients to feel like they knew us and so she'd had us provide photographs and write a bio each. Mine didn't say very much to be honest, nothing more than the fact that I lived locally with Cooper and Watson.

"I-I didn't mean to frighten you, you w-went extremely pale there for a second."

"It's okay, it's not your fault. I'm ever so sorry. So, what can I call you Mr…?"

"It's Peter. P-please just call me Peter."

"Peter," I said, smiling. "Follow me."

The tour I gave Peter was fairly standard. We started in reception. I showed him the treatment rooms. I explained that one was kept for the sole purpose of seeing cats because it helped to reduce their stress levels if they weren't surrounded by the scent of dog. I showed him the overnighters and we peeped in through the window of the surgery. Clients weren't allowed in there because we had to keep everything inside sterile. During the tour I kept up a running commentary about the practice.

"And that's about all there is to see," I concluded brightly after I'd explained the types of surgery that we did on site. "Have you any questions?" I asked. Usually tours were more conversational but Peter had barely said a word. He was either bored rigid, even though he'd asked for the tour, or incredibly shy. I assumed the latter because there had been hints of a stammer once or twice during the tour.

"How long have you worked here?" he asked, which was not an unusual question. Potential clients often wanted to know that they wouldn't be seeing an endless stream of new faces.

"Me? Erm, I've been here for…" I did a quick calculation "…about seven years now. Blimey, that's flown, it doesn't feel like so long."

"And is Andrew a good man to work for?"

That's an odd question, I thought. "He's great, he's a superb vet. He loves the animals."

"But does he treat you well?" Peter persisted. "You can tell a lot about a man by how he treats his staff. I-I just want to make sure I'm using the best."

That makes a bit more sense, my internal voice piped up. "He treats me like I'm a part of his family," I reassured.

"I-Is there a toilet I could use?" Peter asked, abruptly changing the subject. "I'm sorry, weak bladder," he concluded a little bit lamely.

"Sure, this way." I said, leading Peter back to our break room. "It's just through there," I indicated.

While I waited for Peter, I checked on Jessica and Fletcher. Now that they had been officially adopted by Cedar's Veterinary Centre they usually had the run of the break room and the apartment upstairs, but while the open day was on they were back in their playpen. And they were not happy about it.

Both of them came running, mewling loudly to be let out when they saw that it was me. Which would have made me feel special if it wasn't for the fact that I knew they would have done exactly the same if it was Ellie or Andrew or anyone else alive that had entered the break room. Fickle little devils.

It was impossible to choose between the two of them and so I scooped them both up for a snuggle.

"Hey sweet peas," I said, kissing each of them on the top of their heads. "Miss me?" I asked, knowing full well that I was anthropomorphising but not caring. They both purred in response and Fletcher stretched his paw up and patted my face. God bless him.

I heard a noise behind me and turned to see Peter returning from the bathroom.

"Aren't they adorable?" I asked.

"Oh... erm, yes adorable." He replied, albeit he seemed a little reluctant.

"Come and say hello, they won't bite... much."

Warily Peter stepped closer. For someone thinking about getting a cat he was exhibiting some odd behaviour. He hadn't seemed overly interested during the tour and he seemed almost afraid of the kittens.

"Honestly, they won't bite," I reiterated, wondering if he'd taken my joke seriously.

Seemingly with some reluctance Peter reached to stroke Fletcher who was closest to him, but in perfect synchronicity both of the kittens shrank away from him hissing with such venom that even I was taken aback, and I knew that they could be little beasts.

"Goodness, they don't normally do that," I apologised. "Jessica! Fletcher! Stop that. Naughty toe-rags," I chastised.

"It's fine," Peter said, hurriedly stepping back. "Maybe a cat isn't for me," he finished.

"Oh, don't let these two put you off," I replied, putting them both back in their playpen. "They've only ever known us here at the vets, they're just a little shy with strangers." I said, but even as I offered my explanation, I knew it wasn't quite the truth. Neither Jessica nor Fletcher had ever shown any signs of shyness. True, they could be aggressive but they were also loving and playful.

"I'd better let you get on with things anyway," Peter said, retreating to the door of the break room. I followed and saw him to the front door of the practice, a little bit bemused by my unusual tour guest.

CHAPTER 10 – EMMA

Sunday 10th February 2019

"So, what exactly do you mean by a 'dark blue sedan'?" my Dad asked.

The open day had finished and our clients had gone home, the reception area had been restored to its usual set up and my Dad now felt justified in asking all of his questions. He had behaved himself during the open day and so it was only fair. But did he really have to ask Andrew and Marie if they would be a part of the conversation? Of course he did! And so we hadn't even left the veterinary centre before the grilling commenced. Apparently I no longer had a say in who got to know that I was being stalked. His argument being that because I spent so much of my time in Andrew's care, Andrew needed to know what was going on so that he could look after me. I'd started to disagree on the grounds that Andrew was just my boss but seeing as how that wasn't altogether true, and because Ellie sided with my Dad, I gave in at pace. I was never going to win an argument against my Dad *and* Ellie.

We, as in me, my parents, my brother Scott, Andrew and Marie *and* Ellie and her parents were all squeezed into the break room. I had centre stage and was stood leaning against the kitchen units while everyone else was sat or perched on one of the four armchairs that usually circled the coffee table, all of which had been turned to face me. There wasn't really enough room for eight people to sit comfortably, partly because of Jessica and Fletcher's pen and partly because the room simply wasn't big enough, but no-one moved.

The rest of the staff had all been waved off a while ago, perhaps a little bit suspicious as to why my Dad was insistent that a select few remain behind but gone nonetheless. Jessica and Fletcher had been freed and then my trial had begun. The room even resembled a courtroom, if you squinted a little bit and had a really good imagination.

My Dad's cross examination had focused mostly on the car, about which there was not a lot I could say.

"You know, a dark blue car," I answered as sarcastically as I could manage. "As in one that's dark blue in colour."

My Dad didn't even try to hide his growing frustration with me, his jaw clenching tightly.

"Emma, that is not helpful," my Mum interjected calmly, laying a hand on my Dad's leg. She had the pleasure of being seated properly in one of the armchairs with my snarky Dad perched next to her. "Your father wants to know the make and model of the car and you know it."

"I don't know the make or model of the car. I know jack shit about cars. You know that!" I rarely swore, let alone around my parents, but my Dad's questions were relentless and I was starting to get irritated.

"Okay, well let's start with why you keep calling it a sedan," my Mum continued, her tone remaining even. "That's an American term so why a 'sedan'?"

"Is it? An American term I mean? Huh, I didn't know that."

"Yes, it's American. We have saloons, Americans have sedans. Is it a saloon that you've been seeing?"

"I don't know, what's a saloon?" I asked, while my Dad clenched his jaw some more.

"Our car is a saloon," he interjected quite firmly.

"Oh, it's not one of those then," I answered glancing at Ellie as she hid a smile.

"Okay, so in fact it's not a sedan at all?" my Mum persisted. "Whose car does it look most like?"

"Erm…" my Mum was good, other than earlier when I had suddenly realised that Charlotte drove a dark blue sedan (which I now knew was not a sedan at all!) I'd never stopped to wonder if the car that I kept seeing looked anything like the car of anyone I knew. I didn't pay much attention to cars though. Really it was a miracle that I'd even picked up on the fact I was being followed. My knowledge of, and interest in, cars was so limited that even my driving instructor had had to resort to directing me by anything other than the other cars on the road. My irritation waned.

"It's definitely not as big as Andrew's car…" I stated, looking towards him. He inclined his head slightly encouraging me to go on. Andrew drove an older Land Rover and while the newer ones were all starting to blend together, I could confidently say that it wasn't that big. I didn't know cars but I could identify a Land Rover. "But it's bigger than Ellie's..." which was a given really because she drove a Fiat 500 and they were tiny. "And it stands up more than yours does..." I continued, looking back towards my Mum. "I guess mostly it looks like Charlotte's car," I concluded. "Or Matthew's," I added, because they did drive identical cars.

"So, in old money it's a hatchback."

"What do you mean by 'in old money'?" I asked, my curiosity piqued.

"Emma," my Mum sighed, "you really don't pay attention to anything around you, do you?" she asked, no doubt expecting me to argue against her. My family firmly believed that I wandered through the world oblivious to what went on around me. It wasn't true but I'd never been able to persuade them of the facts. The fact was that I did pay attention to lots of things but only those things that interested me. Cars did not interest me ergo I did not pay attention to them. Usually my Mum's comment would have had me arguing against her.

"On this one occasion, let's agree that I don't," I answered, because while I wanted to argue against her for no other reason than the love of a good argument, I wanted to understand what she meant by 'in old money' more. "What do you mean?"

"Really? You agree. After all this time."

"Mum!" I said sharply, my temper flaring again.

My Mum smiled serenely, no doubt believing she'd won, before answering my question, "Nowadays people refer to the bigger hatchbacks as SUVs."

A no-doubt-inappropriate feeling of triumph buzzed inside of me. "Excellent," I answered jubilantly. "Mr. Dark Blue Sedan can become Mr. DBS, as in Mr. Dark Blue SUV then." I felt elated that I didn't really need to re-name my stalker because of course that was an important factor to me. Although judging from the glare that my Dad shot in my direction I might have been the only one that thought as much.

"Shall we move on from the topic of the car?" Scott asked, coming to my rescue and saving me from the growing wrath of our father. "Unless you thought on and took a note of the number plate?" he added innocently.

You bastard! I thought.

"Did you?" my Dad asked hopefully.

"No. But in my defence, I have thought about it. I just haven't done it yet. Recently I've tended to panic whenever I've seen the car," I added, a little wobble in my voice.

"It's okay," my Dad answered softly, all of his anger gone. He stood and pulled me into his arms and I let him.

"I'm sorry Daddy," I whispered to him.

"Don't be sorry. This isn't your fault. We'll sort it out, don't worry."

Over my Dad's shoulder I smirked at my brother. His question had totally backfired. Ha!

"Okay," I said, taking a deep breath and pulling away from my Dad, steeling myself for the next round of questions. "What else do you want to know?"

"Where did the flowers come from?" my Mum asked.

"I don't know exactly. Rhona said that Interflora delivered them." I looked at Andrew.

"That's correct," Andrew nodded in confirmation.

"Interflora uses local florists to fulfil their orders though," my Mum persisted, twisting in her seat to face Andrew.

"Do they?" he asked. And Mum thought I wandered through life oblivious!

My Mum sighed a very audible sigh and turned back to me, "What did you do with them Emma?"

It was Ellie that answered though, "She took them to Grammy. She didn't like the smell."

"Okay, that's good. There must have been a label on them, we can check which florist delivered them."

"Why?" I asked. "How is knowing where the flowers came from going to help?"

"There might be CCTV," my Mum answered confidently. "The police might be able to get an ID of your stalker."

"Maybe in London. Or Manchester."

"You never know."

"I think you've watched too many crime shows on TV Mum."

"There was a card," Ellie added, bringing us back on track. "I grabbed it, I might even still have it in my pocket. It said something about them being for 'the love of my life'. Maybe the florist's name is on that."

"Great! A crazy stalker," I said at the same time that my Mum exclaimed Ellie's brilliance.

"Now, what about the letter? Where's that?" My Mum was on a roll.

"Erm... I'm not really sure. By the phone I guess. After I read it, Ellie made me ring you guys so I guess it just got plonked. But it definitely can't help the police track down the stalker. It was hand-delivered so no post mark and there's nothing in the content to identify who sent it."

"Hmm, maybe you're right," my Mum answered. "But make sure you put it somewhere safe and give it to the police," she added before falling silent.

"Did you ever look at the driver of the car?" Scott asked. "You should have been able to see him in your rear view."

I blushed because I hadn't. I'd never really bothered to look at who was driving the car.

"No," I answered. "No, I don't know what my stalker looks like, I haven't got a note of the number plate, and I don't know where the flowers came from. It was only last night when the letter was delivered that I really accepted I was being stalked. I mean, before that I'd wondered, and sometimes I was even sure about it but I always struggled to believe it." I felt deflated suddenly. "For all I know it could be Charlotte," I added miserably.

"That's an odd thing to say," Marie spoke up for the first time. "Surely you don't think it's anyone here?"

"No, don't be silly, of course not," I reassured. "I know it's no-one in this room. And I know it's not Rhona. Or anyone else that I've worked with for the last seven years. But what do we really know about Charlotte?" I asked, even though I'd dismissed the notion that it could be her earlier on at the open day.

"Em," Ellie chided gently. "It's not Charlotte. Just because she's a little odd it doesn't mean that she's stalking you." Ellie was well aware of what I thought about Charlotte, albeit she wasn't aware that I had briefly wondered if she could be my stalker earlier on that day.

"But what if…" I started to say.

"It's not Charlotte," Ellie reiterated. "And if you really think it could be Charlotte, you must also consider that it might be Matthew."

"Obviously it's not Matthew," I responded. The idea that it could be Matthew was just laughable. He was lovely, everyone thought so.

"Surely we're not really having this conversation about two of our vets, are we?" Marie asked. She sounded incredulous.

"Well, someone's stalking her," my Dad retorted.

"Yes, I get that," Marie answered. "But it's not one of us."

"How do we know that?" Joanne asked. Both of Ellie's parents had remained quiet throughout most of the conversation. They'd murmured their sympathies but they'd left my parents to ask the questions.

"You can't be serious," Marie retorted hotly.

"I am serious. If Ellie was the one being stalked I'd want all avenues explored. We don't know who it is, so we can't say who it isn't."

"By that logic it could literally be anyone, including you."

The tension in the room was evidently rising.

"Enough!" Andrew announced sharply surprising us all. "We will not have this argument. Emma is being stalked. We will do whatever we need to do for her. Woe betide whoever is behind it." He stood and marched out of the room leaving everyone else quiet, stunned into silence.

The seconds ticked by. No-one seemed to know what to say after Andrews explosive departure and a stillness settled in the room. I was shocked because Andrew had raised his voice. It was so unlike him, he was a man of few words, a gentle man.

Eventually it was my Mum who spoke up, "Well, we should all probably go," she said, reaching for her things and making to stand up.

"Yes, absolutely," Joanne agreed, scooting to the edge of her own seat.

My Mums statement galvanised everyone into motion. Scott jumped to his feet, Ellie stretched, Frank stood with Joanne, my Dad, who was still stood with me, pulled me into his side for a quick hug. Only Marie sat still.

"Wait!" she said suddenly. "I just wanted to say that of course Andrew and I will do whatever we need to do to help out here. I'm sorry, I don't believe it's someone who works here but that doesn't mean I don't believe it's happening."

"It's okay Marie," I shrugged. "Don't worry about it."

"No Emma. I do worry about it, about you. Maybe you should take a few days off?" she suggested.

"That's a good idea," my Dad interjected, a little bit too happily. "You could come and spend a few days at home with us."

"No Dad." I shook my head firmly. "And no thank-you Marie."

"But..."

"No Dad. I have a life of my own that I'm very happy with. I'm not going to let some crazy freak ruin it for me."

"Do you want me to stay over?" Ellie asked while everyone gathered their belongings.

"Honestly, no," I answered. "I just want to go home, put my

pyjamas on and climb into bed. I feel completely wiped out."

"Okay, but you know you can't do that. Cooper and Watson will want some play out time. I could just stay for tea."

Damn! Ellie was right. Cooper and Watson didn't have a cat flap and weren't allowed out unless I was home. They would be little demons at bedtime if they didn't get some play out time. That meant I would have to stay up to watch for them coming home. And then I would have to let them out again because they wouldn't have tired themselves out properly. And then in again and then out again. Watson in particular was a little pest. His favourite trick in all the world was to see how many times he could get Mummy to stand up for him in one evening.

"It's okay, really. Me and the sofa will cosy up together. I don't think I have any conversation left in me tonight." I smiled at her. It wasn't a lie but equally it wasn't the entire truth. What I really wanted to do was to talk to Blake, if he was really real and not just a dream that was. Now that the open day was over and everyone was up to speed with my stalking issue I wanted to find out more about him, find out if he was more than just a product of my over-tired imagination. I'd never lied to Ellie before, or even withheld a smidgen of the truth from her, but I didn't know where to start with this one.

"You sure?"

"Yep. I really am. You do need to come home with me though to get your car. Or you can leave it at mine and we'll sort it tomorrow."

"Let's sort it tomorrow. I'll catch a lift home with Mum and Dad, I think Mum will want me at home tonight anyway. It's not only your movements that'll be closely monitored from now on, you know?" She pulled a face and I couldn't help but laugh. She was right, my Dad would want to know where I was every minute of every day now that he knew I was being stalked and her Mum would want to wrap her in cotton wool. Both were worriers. "Thanks," she said, dryly.

"Hey, what are friends for?"

CHAPTER 11 – EMMA

Sunday 10th February 2019

It took a while to extricate myself from Cedar's Veterinary Centre. There were hugs all round and lots of advice. Or it could have been instruction but I was choosing to think of it as advice.

"Don't forget to lock the doors." The front door was a Yale and, as a consequence, my door was always locked.

"And keep them all closed at all times." Because sometimes I left my doors wide open just for the fun of it, especially in the middle of winter.

"Keep your phone near you." It rarely left my side anyway.

"And text me every half an hour." No! Just no. Maybe if that request had come from Ellie but that was one of my Dad's pleas.

"Check under the bed and in all the wardrobes before you go to sleep." Really?

"And ring the police." Okay, that was a sensible piece of advice and I intended to ring them the next day. Rightly or wrongly I assumed that only the emergency staff worked at the weekend and my issue wasn't exactly an emergency. Maybe if I had been threatened or actually harmed but I didn't think receiving a bouquet of roses or a letter justified calling the emergency services. If anything, now that I had accepted I was being stalked, it was creepy rather than scary.

Finally, after many promises to my Dad that I would be absolutely fine, I made it out of the door.

Cooper and Watson, oblivious to what was happening in my world, demanded that their usual treats-tea-and-out routine be maintained when I first got home, and then I had to text everyone to let them know my whereabouts. As a consequence, I didn't have time to think about Blake immediately, but when I did two thoughts occurred. Firstly, that sense of peace that had engulfed me when Blake had slapped me had stayed put. And secondly, I had one-hundred-and-one questions. How did I contact him? Or did I have to wait for him to contact me? Was he really real? Perhaps he was just a dream after all. Or maybe I needed to be asleep for him to show himself. He had said something about me pulling him to me though. Was it that simple? Did I just have to will it and poof he would appear?

"Blake?" I said tentatively, feeling ridiculous and immediately wishing I could take it back. Nothing happened. There was no disturbance in the air, no knock at the door, nothing. "Plonker," I muttered to myself. "Honestly, he's not real."

"I am real," a voice said from behind me. "I told you that last night."

I jumped and whirled around in the direction of the voice.

Blake, the man of my dreams, was stood in the centre of my lounge. He was absolutely gorgeous and most certainly looked real. I reached up and nipped the skin on my arm, wondering why I wasn't overly alarmed by the fact that, for all intents and purposes, a strange man had just materialised out of nowhere in front of my eyes. While my heart was definitely getting a work-out, that was a result of surprise rather than fear.

"Ouch!" I muttered. Blake raised an eyebrow questioningly but didn't comment. "I wanted to check and see if I was indeed awake," I explained, answering the question that hadn't been asked out loud.

"You are awake. I am real," he answered.

"So, erm... do you want a cup of tea or something?" I asked, not really sure what else to say. If Blake was real and I wasn't dreaming and he really was the Grim Reaper as he had suggested the night before, what on earth was I supposed to say to him? I couldn't remember ever being schooled on the accepted protocols for welcoming such an entity into my home.

"Incorporeal being, remember?"

"Incorporeal being? You didn't tell me that last night. What does it even mean?"

"I did. And it means I don't drink tea."

"So, you're what... a ghost? A manifestation?" I persisted.

"I am not a manifestation," Blake snapped, sounding annoyed. "I am the Keeper of Souls," he continued indignantly. "I exist in spirit form only."

"Meaning what exactly?"

He huffed. "Most people can't see me. I…" he started.

"I can see you," I interrupted.

Blake continued as though I hadn't spoken. "I don't taste or smell or touch or feel. I watch. I listen. I reap the souls of the dying."

"Why can you see and hear if you can't use your other senses?" I asked, the fact that I could see him when most people couldn't momentarily laid on one side.

"I don't know. That's just the way it is."

"And you touched my bedding last night. You made quite a big deal about it," I persisted, ignoring Blake's answer to my earlier question.

I thought back to the previous night and Blakc's apparent fascination with my bedding. Mine was just a plain old cotton duvet cover yet it had appeared to hold him spellbound. I mean it was a nice duvet cover, one of my favourites in fact, but it was still just a duvet cover.

"There is that," he inclined his head gracefully. "It seems as though we have a connection, you and I. I can touch you and…"

"Wait!" I held my hand up. We were both stood in the middle of my lounge now, facing each other but separated by about two or three feet. "How do you know you can touch me?" I asked, my suspicions aroused.

"I have stroked your hair and your cheek while you slept."

"Oh my God, none of it was just a dream," I said, crossing to one of the two sofas in my lounge and sinking down onto it. As the truth dawned on me my legs simply gave way. I felt weak and light headed. I didn't believe in the supernatural but somehow I was having a conversation with the Grim Reaper.

"It's the Keeper of Souls," Blake said, interrupting my thoughts.

"What?" I asked, looking up at Blake. He'd turned slightly so that he was stood square on to where I now sat.

"You keep thinking of me as the Grim Reaper but it's the Keeper of Souls. The Grim Reaper is fictional. He doesn't exist."

"Grim Reaper. Keeper of Souls. What's the difference?" I asked. "And for heaven's sake sit down. And seriously, stop reading my mind."

"There is a whole world of difference," Blake answered indignantly. He took a step towards the other sofa and, despite looking uncertain, lowered himself to sit. "The Grim Reaper is a shadowy figure who is universally feared. He hunts the living, ending the lives of those that he deems unworthy by ripping out their souls. He brings pain and devastation to those who cross his path. I, on the other hand, am not responsible for anyone's death nor do I judge anyone's value. I only reap the souls of the dying." He paused, seemingly for breath, and settled further into his seat. "I am sat," he announced joyfully, a slight smile tugging at the corners of his mouth.

"Yes?"

"I thought I could only touch you, and by extension what you were touching. But I am actually seated. I can feel the sofa underneath me." He wiggled comically in his seat.

"Ooh-kay," I answered, struggling with the implications of what it meant for him to be a spirit. I had assumed that because he'd sat last night he'd be able to sit now. "What did you think would happen when you sat down?" I asked.

"I thought I would only appear to be seated."

"Uh-huh," I answered, not fully sure if I understood. "So, who else can see you then?" I asked, jumping back to the earlier thought that I'd parked, seeing as how I wasn't altogether clear on the seated-but-not-sat thing. I thought the answer to the question of who else could see him would at least be easier to comprehend.

"No-one."

"No-one? But you said 'most' people can't see you. The implication being that some people can see you."

"Only you."

"Wow," I exhaled, slumping in my seat, taken aback.

"Maybe I can touch anything that you have ever touched?" Blake speculated aloud but, without knowing how, I was certain that he wasn't really talking to me, instead he was talking to himself. I answered anyway.

"That doesn't make any sense. Why would you be able to touch something just because I've touched it?"

"I don't know. I don't understand any of this either."

"Surely it's more likely," I continued as though he hadn't replied, "that, if we're connected, as you surmise, when you're near me you're made whole."

"I am whole all the time," Blake sounded indignant again.

"Okay," I thought briefly for the right word, "corporeal then."

"Maybe."

"We could easily test the theory. All I would have to do is walk away from you and see if you suddenly fell through the sofa."

"I wouldn't fall through the sofa." Indignant seemed to be Blake's 'go-to' setting.

"We'll see about that, shall we?" I answered sarcastically standing swiftly and walking away from him.

The problem was that my house was on the small side. From front to back it was only about 30 feet in length and I was therefore outside in the back garden before a strange sensation made me shiver and Blake reacted.

"Remarkable," he said, so softly that I nearly missed it. If I was going to spend any time with him I really needed to teach him some conversational manners.

Blake hadn't fallen through the sofa, God damnit! He stood and took a step towards me, becoming physically present again with a peculiar 'pop' that I felt inside of me and stumbling almost immediately on one of the many discarded cat toys that littered my house. You could almost say that one of my hobbies was buying cat toys. It was a futile exercise because neither Cooper nor Watson ever showed any interest in anything other than their scratching post, but I persisted in the vain hope that, at the very least, they took them to be a sign of Mummy's love for them both.

"Being like this may take some getting used to," Blake muttered as he righted himself and straightened his clothes. "I have never had to concern myself with obstacles."

Laughter bubbled up inside of me as the absurdity of the situation hit me. Because it was blowing a gale, I was stood freezing to death in the garden (although hopefully not literally), trying to distance myself from the Grim Reaper (also known as the Keeper of Souls), while he stumbled about inside of my house because, for some reason that neither one of us understood, proximity to me forced him to manifest.

It all got too much and I laughed out loud.

"It's not funny," Blake said joining me outside, his face stern. But as he stepped out of the house a joyous smile lit up his entire face. It was a wonderful smile, one that reached his eyes so that they sparkled brightly, reflecting the light from my house. He spread his arms wide and turned in a circle, the wind lifting his jacket tails and tugging at his shirt. It tousled his hair, whipping the longer strands across his face and in his eyes. It would have annoyed me, in fact it was annoying me because the wind was tugging at my own hair too, but Blake only laughed.

It was my turn to raise an eyebrow questioningly.

"This is wonderful," Blake said, answering my question, his delight obvious. "The wind... the cold, it's... exquisite. I never imagined that it would feel like this. I thought I understood but I didn't. I was wrong. It's so much more."

"It's freezing," I replied dryly, hugging myself tightly, my teeth starting to chatter.

"It's heavenly."

"Nope, it's definitely not heavenly," I answered, "a cooling breeze when the sun shines brightly is heavenly. Plunging into a cold pool on a hot day is heavenly. Ice cold cider in the peak of summer is heavenly. This is just cold." With just my jeans, a long sleeved t-shirt and some pumps on, I was starting to go numb. Without any thought for Blake, I stepped into the house and walked away from the back door into the lounge again. I sensed the exact moment when my sphere of influence failed Blake. It was difficult to explain but there was a definite pop and when I turned to face Blake, he was no longer affected by the wind. His hair lay untouched, curling slightly around his face, his clothes fell straight and darkness pooled around his feet once more.

"I'm sorry," I said, sensing his sadness. "It's too cold for me out there."

"I understand," Blake answered. "I felt it from your perspective too."

I stilled. "What did you just say?" I asked.

"I felt it from your perspective too," Blake repeated, remaining in the garden.

"I felt it from your perspective," I repeated but much slower than Blake. I turned the words over in my mind and thought about what they meant, and what I had just sensed.

"What is it?" Blake asked.

"I think I felt what you were feeling. I felt your sorrow a moment ago." The world fell away for me. There was just Blake and I in all the universe. Him standing in my garden facing into my house, untouched by the wind, unable to feel the cold. Me in my house facing out into my garden, the warmth of the central heating slowly thawing my fingers and toes, causing them to tingle as my blood recirculated.

"I felt your sorrow," I said again, quietly almost to myself.

Blake moved towards me, stepping into the house with a grace and elegance that he did not seem to possess when he was corporeal. I felt a pop and then he took me in his arms, pulling me into him. Blake was much taller than I was and so I was easily able to rest my head against his shoulder. The embroidery of his jacket gave it a coarse feel, but I still snuggled my cheek into him wishing my skin was touching his. I'd dreamed about being in his arms for so long and now that it was happening I wasn't even touching him, feeling him.

"As I said earlier, there is a connection between you and me. I don't understand it but I feel you calling to me, I hear your thoughts…"

I reddened slightly then wondering just how many of my thoughts he had heard.

"All of them, when I am close to you anyway," Blake continued, although whether or not he was responding to my internal musings was unclear. "I feel what you're feeling too. And perhaps you are now starting to feel what I feel, perhaps in time you will also be able to hear my thoughts."

I pulled away, confused about everything. "But why, why is this happening? Who am I to you? I'm nobody. How can I possibly be connected to you? I didn't even believe you existed until just now. Hell, I'm still not sure if I believe you exist. Maybe you're an elaborate hallucination."

"I can promise you that I'm not a hallucination. I don't know how to prove it to you, but I am as real as you are. I just exist on a different plane normally." Blake paused for breath. "But as to why this is happening or who you are, I don't know. All I can tell you is that you are the most beautiful woman I have ever seen in the whole of my life, and I have lived a very long life. From the moment that I first heard your call I've yearned for you. I've tried to deny it, I've tried to ignore you, resist you. I've even been angry with you but the truth is I've never wanted anyone as much as I've wanted you. Being incorporeal has never been such a burden until now."

Suddenly it felt extremely hot. Despite the fact that I didn't know him, despite the fact that he was apparently the stuff of myth and legend, I wanted Blake. And he, it seemed, wanted me too.

"I do want you," Blake answered my thoughts again. "Of all the things in all the world that I could experience, what I would like most of all is to touch you, to stroke you... perhaps even to kiss you... if you'd let me."

My heart skipped a beat. Suddenly I didn't care why this was happening or even if Blake was a product of my imagination, a hallucination that my tired mind had created. All I cared about was feeling his lips pressed against my own, his tongue in my mouth and his hands on my body. And then he was kissing me, gently at first but with an increasing degree of urgency. He pressed his body into mine, pulling me even closer to him while sliding his hands underneath my long sleeved t-shirt. And with that I blacked out.

CHAPTER 12 – BLAKE

Sunday 10th February 2019

Blake stood with Emma in his arms. His mental shields started to crumble and his endless icy rage started to thaw as his lips pressed against hers. He wasn't alone. For the first time in his life he was finally with someone and not just Seith.

Blake had never kissed anyone before but he instinctively understood the mechanics of kissing, he knew to gently press his lips against hers and to rest his hands on her waist before drawing her into him. He marvelled at the texture of Emma's t-shirt as he pulled her closer, claiming her as his own. He savoured the silken feel of her lips for as long as he could before needing more and gently probing for her tongue with his own. And then he felt her go limp in his arms.

Briefly he wondered if he'd crushed her but on searching through his stolen memories, he realised that she'd simply blacked out. Odd. He continued to search his stolen memories as he gently laid her on the ground and mentally called for Seith. It did not seem all that common for people to black out when they were kissed but then again, Emma was the first person that he had ever kissed. Maybe he'd inadvertently started to reap her soul. He had tasted the sweetness of her breath, maybe that had been her soul.

And then he too started to feel dizzy. Being corporeal was not all that it was cracked up to be.

Seith had appeared the instant that Blake had called and had sat beside Emma's body even before Blake could give any kind of instruction, seemingly knowing that Emma was in danger.

"Seith, stand guar…" Blake said, his voice growing thick, before he too collapsed. His body fell next to Emma's, his arm draped possessively across her middle.

Blake's last conscious thought as his eyesight dimmed was to curse that he had only just started to live his life. Why had he not acted sooner when she had first called to him? Weeks had been wasted, months even.

Blake lay in darkness for a while before realising that he was awake. How long he'd lain there, wherever there was, he didn't know. It could have been seconds; it could have been hours. But slowly he came around.

At first, his eyes were worse than useless, the darkness all consuming. And he heard nothing. Eventually though, he detected the occasional sound, words maybe. In time, his ears picked out more and more and then finally the darkness relented. Wisps of grey flickered around him, slowly solidifying into shapes.

Blake tentatively sat. He still felt dizzy, his head hurt and his mouth was so dry that it felt like it was covered in fur. The fact that he felt all of those things barely registered though, his only concern was for Emma. He sensed that she was nearby but he couldn't see her. Nor could he feel her with outstretched arms.

"Emma?" He called her name while standing, hoping that she'd answer or that he'd find her body.

As he raised himself to his full height the wisps of grey that had been slowly solidifying into shapes resolved themselves at last. Blake gasped. He was looking at Emma in the arms of another man. But it wasn't Emma. With his head throbbing as it was, his brain worked slowly to pick out the differences. First of all the look-alike was wearing strange clothes. Blake had only ever seen Emma in trousers or pyjama's, this woman was dressed in a long, woollen skirt with a blouse tucked in at her waist and a shawl wrapped around her shoulders. The blouse was pale in colour, white but not quite white, and both the skirt and the shawl were dark brown, colours that Emma had never worn because Emma favoured the red-blue spectrum. Secondly, the look-alike was older, leaner. The plumpness of Emma's face had been replaced with a much harder profile. And she was shorter than Emma. Emma was tall and curvaceous, she had a lushness about her, a ripeness that was missing in the look-alike.

In spite of the differences, the similarities were uncanny. The look-alike's features, despite being comparatively pinched, were Emma's. The look-alike's eyes were a precise match. And her hair was the exact same shade of copper. The only difference there was how Emma and the look-alike wore it: the look-alike had her hair securely pinned at the nape of her neck in a tight bun whereas Emma tended to wear her hair loose or in a ponytail.

Blake did not recognise the man but he studied his face intently. He was a bulky man, with plain features. His hair had been cropped short and he had the beginnings of a beard. He was marginally taller than Emma's look-alike but he wasn't a tall man. It was evident that he had the strength of an ox but he held the look-alike with such tenderness and gentility.

Blake felt no shame about his voyeurism. He'd lived his whole life watching others, two more meant nothing to him. But if it hadn't been for the look-a-like he would have left them alone and continued his search for Emma. As it was though, he couldn't tear his eyes away from the scene in front of him.

"Please, let me go John," the look-alike said, doing her best to push away from the man's embrace, despite his obvious dominance.

"I can't. Don't do this to me Bronwyn. I love you, I can't live without you," John responded, tightening his grip on Bronwyn. What had moments before looked like a loving gesture quickly became something else.

Blake thought he understood. A lover's quarrel.

"You have to let me go," Bronwyn said, continuing to fight against John. "Please," she sobbed, tears falling openly from her eyes, running down the side of her face and wetting her cheeks. She was obviously distraught.

"No, I won't. I know you love me too. Why are you doing this?"

"I have to. I do love you, but I want more than you can give me."

"A child," John replied sadly, releasing Bronwyn from his grip at last, his hands falling uselessly to his side, his head bowing in grief. He looked defeated, beaten. "You want a child more than you want me," he whispered.

"I'm sorry my love. My body aches to be a mother and I can never have that while I am with you. You do not give life, you take it away. That is your duty and I understand, I really do, but you must let me go. You must let me have a normal life."

Blake was startled by Bronwyn's last statement. Was her lover a murderer? Or did she think he was the Keeper of Souls? But that couldn't be. Blake was the Keeper of Souls, the only Keeper of Souls. He'd searched for others like him, he'd wanted there to be more like him, but he'd never found any. He'd long since concluded that he was the only one.

John raised himself up to his full height and took a deep breath. "That's not entirely true, there is one life that is mine to give," he said.

A look of confusion crossed Bronwyn's face. Blake might have missed it if he hadn't seen the exact same look on Emma's face so very often in the last 24 hours. He watched as understanding dawned.

"No!" Bronwyn exclaimed, her hands reaching to John, imploring him not to do whatever it was he was intent on doing. "Please no," she begged. "Don't do this, not for me. Don't sacrifice yourself."

"It is no sacrifice my love," John answered calmly, his voice steely. He was clearly resolved on a particular course of action but Blake had no idea what that might be. "Without you my life is not worth living, let me give you what you want." And with that he stepped back from Bronwyn and very slowly, very deliberately, reached into himself, pushing his hand firmly into his chest. Blake could not ascertain how he did it but he clearly saw John's hand pass into his own body.

At first Blake did not understand what he was seeing, what he was being allowed to witness, but then he too understood. John reached into himself and withdrew his own soul. Blake didn't even know such a thing was possible but, as John pulled his hand free, Blake could clearly see that he held a golden substance tightly within his grasp. It ebbed and flowed, drawn always back to the body from whence it came, yearning to be back inside of its carrier.

Bronwyn screamed as John thrust his soul at her pushing it into her abdomen. She collapsed on the ground screaming some more as the soul was absorbed into her body. John too collapsed then.

"I love you Bronwyn. I'll always love you. Please don't forget me," he said weakly.

"John, oh John," Bronwyn sobbed, crawling to his side. She pulled him into her lap and cradled his head and upper body with her own. "I love you so much my darling, of course I'll never forget you." She bent to kiss him, tears streaming openly down her face. As her lips met his, his body started to disintegrate. Blake watched as it crumbled into nothing more than dust. A handful of particles the colour of sunshine rose into the surrounding air, sparkling brightly as they caught the light.

CHAPTER 13 – EMMA

Monday 11th February 2019

There was a definite weight on my chest when I woke up. My breathing was shallow and despite all of my attempts to fill my lungs with air, I simply couldn't. I opened my eyes a crack and jumped.

Watson's little pink nose was mere millimetres from my own, his golden-green unblinking eyes staring straight into mine. That explained the weight on my chest then. At least it wasn't Cooper who had decided to settle there. Cooper was much bigger than his brother, I might have been in serious trouble if he'd been the one on top of me.

"Watson," I said with a sigh, pulling myself into a half-seated position. "Mummy can't breathe properly when you do that. And we don't have to get up today, it's my day off, remember?" Because after the open day we all got a day off (apart from the emergency cover).

Watson slid down from my chest and into my lap, nestling there quite happily, purring loudly. He immediately started kneading, bunching the quilt cover up around him. It was the same one that Blake had been fascinated with, crisp white cotton with dark purple flowers embroidered across the middle. If Watson continued to knead it so enthusiastically I doubted it would last much longer.

"You're awake," Blake announced and I jumped again. I hadn't exactly forgotten about him, but I hadn't been expecting to see him either. He stood, as usual, in the corner of my bedroom cloaked in shadow. The sun was yet to rise judging from the gloominess of my bedroom, and if he hadn't spoken I wouldn't have even known he was there.

"Am I still dreaming?" I asked.

"We've covered this already. You're not dreaming."

"Uh-huh," I answered sleepily snuggling back down in my bed. "Not dreaming," I muttered, closing my eyes. But as I closed them an image of a woman who looked a lot like me rose unbidden in my mind's eye. She was crumpled on the floor, a man in her arms, and she was sobbing. I assumed therefore that the man had died. As I watched, the woman bent to kiss his body but it disintegrated as she laid her lips on his. Golden coloured specks of dust rose up into the air around them casting off such a bright light that I'd had to look away.

My memory of the previous evening came flooding back to me. Blake had answered my call, we'd learned that proximity to me gave him substance somehow, he'd felt the wind and the cold and had been delighted by them. I'd discovered that I could sense his emotions and then... he'd kissed me. I smiled as my memory returned. As our lips had met he'd crushed his body into mine pulling me so close that I'd... blacked out.

"I blacked out?" I asked quizzically pulling myself all the way up into a seated position. Poor Watson! "Then how did I…" I gestured around my bedroom at my bed. The last thing I remembered was kissing him in the lounge but I'd woken in my own bed.

"I carried you," Blake answered. "I took off your shoes and your jeans but left you clothed otherwise."

Only then did I realise that I was wearing yesterday's t-shirt instead of my pyjamas. A heat rose within me. Blake had seen me in my underwear. Desperately I tried to remember which set I had on. I prayed it was one of the nicer ones.

"I tried not to look. But they are purple, like your bedroom. Very nice."

"Oh," I answered, blushing. At least they were nice ones, although I wouldn't have said they were like my bedroom. My bedroom was painted the palest colour of purple that I'd been able to find when I'd bought the house. I'd finished the room with white furniture, mostly white bedding and curtains that were as dark in colour as the paint was light. Over time, I'd added a throw and some cushions to the bed for extra depth and texture. My underwear, in comparison, was a bluey shade of purple with a dark pink floral pattern on them.

Blake fell silent and my mind wandered, still trying to make sense of everything that had happened, not only in the last 24 hours but in the last few months. The dreams that I had been having of Mr. TDH were really of Blake and they weren't really dreams, he had been standing in my bedroom, he had stroked my hair, he had stroked my cheek, I really had seen him, both in my lounge and at the Trafford Centre. And he had come to me the other night, we'd talked and he'd told me he was the Keeper of Souls. And then the night before... we'd kissed.

"What do you remember?" Blake asked suddenly, interrupting my thoughts. "Tell me."

"Can't you... you know?" I twirled my fingers by the side of my head.

"I can. But your thoughts are racing. Talk to me, maybe that way you'll start to make sense of everything." He took a step towards my bed, seemingly uncertain.

"Why aren't you sitting?" I asked. A tiny shiver ran down my spine because I realised that he was acting 'off'. It was very subtle but Blake was usually stern and foreboding, he never acted like he was unsure of anything. But now, his tone of his voice alternated, half of the time he sounded kind and gentle but half of the time he sounded abrupt and harsh. He seemed conflicted and, as the word came to me, I felt it. His emotions swept over me like an ocean crashing over the tide barrier on a stormy day.

"I... uhm... I don't know if I caused you — us — to black out."

"You blacked out too?" I asked, my voice soft, barely more than a whisper. My thoughts were racing but one thing was clear to me. "Come, sit. Even if you did cause it, it only happened when we kissed. Maybe we just can't do that anymore," I said, but my heart plummeted at the thought of never kissing Blake ever again. It had been everything I'd dreamed it would be and more. I reached up unconsciously and brushed my fingers over my lips, remembering the sensation from before, of his lips against mine. I sighed just as Blake finally sat at the foot of my bed.

"For God's sake Blake, just sit down," I snapped although I wasn't really angry with Blake, just disappointed that I might never be in his arms again. Blake settled where he sat. He didn't look completely comfortable.

"You look miserable," I said.

"I feel much of what you feel," he replied.

"Then kiss me again, what's the worst that can happen? We black out? Big deal. I've had worse." Hope bubbled up inside of me.

"I can't. I thought I'd started to reap your soul."

Ah-ha that explained the abject misery and why he was hovering. I hadn't pegged Blake for a hoverer. "Is that even possible?" I asked, my curiosity aroused. "You said before that you don't decide who dies, you just reap the souls of the dying. Well, I'm not dying," I concluded. The logic made perfect sense to me and without thinking I reached for him and pulled him towards me, using his jacket as leverage. Watson slipped from between us just as our lips met. We both stilled for a moment but when nothing untoward happened Blake reached behind me, slid his hands underneath my bottom and lifted me into his lap. I wrapped my legs around his waist and then lost myself in our passionate embrace. It was the most exquisite moment of my life. Blake pulled me into him and kissed me with such fervour. His tongue explored my mouth while his hands slid up my back, caressed my neck and eventually settled on stroking my hair.

Eventually we broke for air. "I love your hair," Blake commented.

"Mmm," I purred. "Me too," I replied actually meaning that I loved his hair. Either way it wasn't a lie, I loved my own hair too. I was totally vain about it.

We sat for a while facing each other with me still in Blake's lap, not speaking, not kissing, just being with each other, lost in each other. My body was singing in absolute delight but then I shivered.

"You're getting cold?" Blake asked rhetorically, standing and lifting me in his arms all in one seamless movement. Quickly he settled me under the covers.

"Aren't you getting in?" I asked.

"No, we need to talk," Blake answered as he sat on my bed on top of the covers and pulled me into his arms. We nestled together, me under the covers and him on top of them.

"What do you remember about your vision?" Blake asked.

"My vision?" I repeated.

"Yes, when you blacked out, you had a vision. What do you remember of it?"

I hadn't realised that the woman I'd seen had been part of a vision. I'd just assumed it was all part of a dream, or just my imagination.

"I keep telling you, it's not a dream," Blake said. I could tell that he was trying to be patient but he didn't quite succeed in pulling it off, a note of irritation was evident in his voice. "Now, what do you remember?"

I thought hard for a few moments and then recounted what I had seen. The woman who looked so much like me, the man who had reached into himself and pulled something from within him, his death and lastly the golden particles. "What do you think it means?" I finished.

"Seith and I discussed it while you were sleeping. I came around much quicker than you did."

"Who is Seith?" I asked.

"That's not important. What's important is what the vision means. Seith says you need to know, I have to tell you." I sensed that without Seith's intervention, whoever he (or she) was, Blake would have kept whatever he'd learned to himself.

"Okay, what does it mean?" I asked cautiously.

"The woman is your ancestor."

"Well, I'd worked that out," I interjected a little bit sarcastically. The woman that I'd seen not only looked like me, she looked like both of the stranger's faces that I'd seen in the mirror recently. A strange feeling crept over me, I felt like I almost knew what Blake was about to say.

"The man," Blake continued, ignoring the fact that I had spoken at all, "was a Keeper of Souls. Perhaps the original Keeper of Souls but certainly the Keeper of Souls that immediately predates me. What you saw, what we both saw, was his death and my birth."

"What?" I exclaimed. Maybe I hadn't known what Blake had been going to say after all.

"I thought I was the only one. I thought I'd only ever been the only one but my memories do not start until the year 1027."

"And what has this got to do with me?"

"You have my soul," Blake answered absently.

"I beg your pardon," I said, sitting upright in the bed. "I have your what did you say?"

Blake pulled me back into him as he answered. "My soul, a part of it anyway. It's obvious. John was in love with Bronwyn but couldn't have a child with her."

"Yes, I got that too," I said, seeing again the defeated slump of John's shoulders when he realised what it was that Bronwyn wanted, a child of her own.

"You obviously don't understand though. John sacrificed himself for Bronwyn so that she could have a child, his child. When he reached inside of himself, he pulled his own soul from his body. That was the golden substance that you saw."

"Eugh," I muttered.

Blake's reply was stern, "The soul is the most beautiful substance in all the world. But it needs a carrier. When John thrust his soul into Bronwyn, giving her his soul, her body created a child for the soul to reside within. She would have died otherwise."

I understood some parts of what Blake was saying but other parts of it eluded me. "But we're talking about John's soul, not your soul. How have I got your soul? And none of what you've said explains why you believe we saw your birth."

Blake sighed. He was not the most patient of teachers. "You have John's soul because souls are passed down through the generations of a family. Bronwyn's child must have gone on to have children, who in turn had children of their own until the day that you were born and the soul, John's soul, was transferred into you. But no human child can contain the Keeper of Souls' soul. That is why you saw my birth and why I said you only have a part of my soul. When John thrust his soul into Bronwyn, her body did what was necessary and created a child, but part of the soul escaped. If you had been paying attention you would have noticed it in the vision, little dust motes danced in the air when John's body disintegrated. Those pieces of the soul came together to create my soul, to create me. We both carry parts of John's soul. You have part of my soul."

"Or you have part of my soul?" I suggested, still working through what Blake had explained. He was usually a man of few words but his explanation had been quite the monologue.

"No, a human child should have been given a human soul. You have my soul," he paused and then added, albeit grudgingly, "although if it makes you feel any better Seith says that you were right when you said that you make me whole."

"Oh my God, the door!" I exclaimed suddenly remembering that Blake had not shut it when he'd come back into the house.

"I locked up last night. And Seith has been standing guard."

"Just who is Seith?" I demanded, wanting to know the answer to that little mystery, but then a new thought dawned. "Oh no, my Dad is going to be so freaked out. And Ellie. She'll kill me. I was supposed to text them before going to bed." I threw back the covers, scrambling to get out of bed.

"Your phone is on charge," Blake said calmly. "That's where you normally leave it so that's where I put it."

The fact that Blake knew where I normally left my phone didn't even register as I unlocked it. Only 23 text messages and two missed calls. I thought there would have been more missed calls. *Thanks Mum.* There was no doubt in my mind that she had been responsible for keeping my Dad at bay.

Everyone had texted but my Dad and Ellie had been the most prolific texters. Dad had sent nine and Ellie had sent five but in essence both of them wanted to know the same thing, that I was alive and well. I sent them both a quick reply: *I'm SO sorry, I fell asleep. Yesterday was a long day and I was tired. I'll call in a few. Xx*

Almost immediately I received two replies:

Mum says I am not allowed to tell you off. Okay, Dad was not happy.

If anyone needed a good night's sleep it was you. Do you want me to come over? Xx Ellie was much more forgiving.

I replied to Ellie but not my Dad. *Can you give me a couple of hours to get my brain into gear? Xx*

Again she replied almost immediately. *Okay, don't bother to call, call your Dad instead, I bet he's going mental :-) I'll see you about 11am. Mum's going to drop me off. Don't forget to ring the police between now and then. Xx*

I looked at the time and was surprised to see it was now 08:37. I never slept that late. The gloominess from earlier on had grudgingly given way and it was now quite bright in my bedroom. "I'm going for a shower," I said to Blake, deciding that I needed time on my own. Seeing the time had awoken my desire to pee!

CHAPTER 14 – EMMA

Monday 11th February 2019

After peeing for an eternity, I stood facing the mirror in my bathroom. I'd consciously avoided all reflective surfaces for the last three days, but the vision I'd shared with Blake had started me thinking and not just about everything he'd told me. What if the stranger's faces that I'd seen in place of my own were somehow a part of all of this, whatever 'this' was? My mind was a jumbled welter of confused thoughts.

Standing in nothing more than my grubby t-shirt and my underwear, I stared at my own face, willing it to change. My hair was tousled from my night-time adventures, and I had make-up smudges underneath my eyes. To be honest, someone else's face might have been nicer to look at!

I concentrated on what I was hoping for, pushing everything else to one side. Either of the faces that I'd seen would have suited me just fine, all I wanted was proof that they hadn't been hallucinations.

"Please," I muttered, scrunching my own face up to close off my vision and then opening my eyes quickly. What I saw in the mirror made me to gasp out loud.

"Are you alright?" Blake shouted. Although whether he'd heard my sharp intake of breath or felt the spike of adrenaline that shot through me wasn't clear.

"Yes, I'm fine. Don't come in here!" I commanded. I needed some time to process what I was seeing.

Staring back at me wasn't just one face. Instead there were many faces, one in front of the other, each overlapping another. I could see them all in the same way that you would see a line of people if you stood slightly off to the side.

The face at the front of the 'queue' was the first face that I'd seen in place of my own. And the last one was face number two. In between, there were at least a dozen more. They all looked like each other and they all looked like me.

My ancestors, I thought. It seemed so obvious all of a sudden that I didn't know why the thought hadn't occurred before.

I studied the first face closely doing a mental compare and contrast until it dawned on me who I was looking at. It was a younger version of Bronwyn, it could only have been her daughter, the first child to carry part of John's soul. I then realised exactly what it was that I was seeing. I was seeing all of those who had ever carried the soul before me, my soul. Or Blake's soul if he was to be believed.

Bronwyn's daughter, and all the other faces, smiled at me and I knew I'd discovered the truth of the situation. Of course, they were probably just mimicking my own smile but I didn't think that was the case.

"Well then," I said aloud, "that means that you…" I nodded slightly at the last face in the queue "…must have been my grandmother. You died just before I was born." A sense of sadness washed over me at the loss of a grandparent I'd never even known. "None of this explains how Grammy could you see though," I added thoughtfully. "And even if she could see you, how did she know you?" As far as I was aware Grammy had never met my grandmother. "Blake!" I called.

I expected him to knock on the bathroom door and ask what it was that I wanted. Or, to just shout through the door. Of course, I failed to take into account the fact that A. He was the Grim Reaper Extraordinaire and B. He had zippo in the way of social skills. Instead of doing either of the things I expected, he materialised behind me. One minute I was alone, the next he was there. I jumped out of my skin and my heart set off galloping in the direction of a new life.

"You're frightened," he declared.

"Well doh!" I answered. "Most people knock." Having Blake in my life was going to take some getting used to.

"I am not most people," he answered blandly.

I shrugged off my mounting anger with some difficulty because I knew — even though I hadn't known him for that long — that Blake simply would not understand my frustration.

"Can you see the faces in the mirror?" I asked, feeling insanely proud of myself for managing to unclench my teeth long enough to ask the question.

Blake took a moment before nodding.

"And?" I prompted, turning away from the mirror to face him. My bathroom was sized for my house and, as a consequence, it was not really designed for two people. A very inappropriate rush of heat spread through my whole body.

"And what?"

"Do you know them?" I asked, the heat dissipating as quickly as it had risen. *Oh my God, it's like trying to draw blood from a stone,* I thought to myself.

"That's not possible."

"What? You don't know them?" I was puzzled by his response.

"No, I don't. But I meant that it's not possible to draw blood from a stone."

"Why would you…" I started to ask before I realised what had happened. Blake had answered my unspoken thought. Again. "Would you knock that off? And how come you don't know them? Don't you know everyone who's ever lived?"

"Why would I know everyone who's ever lived?"

"Because you reaped their souls when they died didn't you?" It seemed obvious to me.

"I reap hundreds of souls a day, I don't remember them all."

"Huh," I responded thinking that nugget of information through. Apparently I still had a lot to learn. "I can't wait to talk to Ellie about all of this," I announced excitedly.

"Who's Ellie?"

"My best friend. I'm surprised you haven't seen me with her."

"The blonde?" Blake asked.

"Yes, that's Ellie. She's going to be blown away by everything that I've learned."

"You can't tell her anything."

"What? Why?"

"Because I said not to."

"That's not really a reason is it? Besides, what are you going to do to stop me from telling her anything?" I asked, deciding that I'd had enough of him. Blake was absolutely without a doubt the most gorgeous man I'd ever laid eyes on, but oh my goodness he was as frustrating as hell. I reached behind him to open the bathroom door and not-so-gently guided him out of my personal space. I needed to pee again. Women! We were a bad design.

"I'm going to tell her whether you like it or not," I declared, sometime later, emerging from the bathroom after I had luxuriated in a long, hot shower. "Obviously it's your choice if you decide to show yourself. It's not like I can make you do anything," I said, trying hard not to wonder if that was true because I knew Blake was listening to my thoughts as well as hearing my words.

And idly, while I'd been in the shower, I had wondered if I could make him do more than just manifest. Did he appear when I called because he wanted to or because he had to? And if being close to me was all it took to make him whole, what else could I make him do?

"You didn't have to wait on the landing," I added, brushing past him in nothing more than a fluffy white towel. He appeared to have loitered just outside of the bathroom door.

"I like being corporeal."

"You could have gone into the bedroom though, or downstairs. Yesterday my…" I paused briefly while I searched for the right word, "…reach was about 30 feet."

"It's less today."

"Oh," I sighed. I couldn't really think of anything else to say to that. I couldn't imagine living my whole life without being able to do anything, it seemed an awful way to live.

"I don't need your sympathy," he declared, even though I hadn't said anything out loud.

"Stop it! Stop reading my mind."

"I'm not reading your mind. Not exactly." Blake paused before confessing that he didn't know how to stop whatever it was that he was not doing. "I don't know how not to hear your thoughts. How do you not hear something?" He had a point and so I moved on.

"Why does my… bubble…" I tried out a new word as a way to articulate whatever it was that I could do to him (or perhaps for him) "…change size?"

"I suspect it is linked to your emotions. It's almost non-existent when you are asleep."

He'd almost joined me in my bedroom and was stood leaning against the door frame, watching me while I prepared for the day ahead. Modestly and without me prompting him, not out loud anyway, he turned his back as I pulled on some clothes. I picked out my sexiest underwear, a black lacy number with a small purple bow on the bottom, an extremely clingy purple t-shirt that had a very deep 'v' at its neckline, and figure hugging jeans. Just in case. And yes, I liked purple.

"There," I said in due course, smoothing out the bedding and opening the curtains. Daylight streamed in through the window flooding my room with bright light. For now at least it looked like a reasonable day.

"Very nice," Blake replied, but he wasn't talking about the bedding or the sunshine. I felt a tingle of lust ripple through me as he eyed me up and down and I knew he was talking about me.

Score one to Emma, I thought smugly.

"She won't be able to see me anyway," Blake continued, changing the subject back to our debate.

"I think you're wrong. She'll be able to see you as long as you're close enough to me. And I was right about the kiss so I'm right about this."

"You're not right about this." Blake's indignation was back. "And you were lucky with the kiss. What if we'd blacked out again?"

"But we didn't."

"No. Seith thinks that we only blacked out because it was the first time that the two parts of my soul had been together since being parted."

"Again, who is Seith?" I asked, ignoring Blake's reference to 'his' soul despite my annoyance.

"My associate."

"Oh, just like Ellie is my associate." I used his word purposely because Ellie was much more than an associate. "If you can talk to Seith then I can talk to Ellie, who's here by the way," I concluded having heard a car pull up outside.

And right on cue she shouted up the stairs, "Em, you up there? Mum says hi."

"I'm coming," I replied as I flounced past Blake and down the stairs to greet Ellie, who had long since had her own key to my house.

"Tea?" she asked, not waiting for me but making herself at home instead.

"Yes please. And what's that smell?" I asked because she'd definitely wafted in enveloped in the scent of something very enticing, something baked.

"Fresh croissants." Ellie replied. "Courtesy of Mum. In case you haven't had breakfast."

"I haven't, not yet anyway." I took a seat at my own dining table while Ellie busied herself in my kitchen.

"Jam or chocolate spread?" she asked, turning and looking at me properly for the first time since she'd arrived. "Wow, you look amazing!" she exclaimed.

You do look good, Blake said in the depths of my mind obviously ear-wigging from upstairs. That was new, he'd never spoken to me telepathically before.

"Any particular reason?" Ellie asked, joining me at the table with a tray full of croissants, jam and chocolate spread.

"I just, you know, felt like making an effort," I answered evasively while she fetched the tea. "I've got loads to tell you, I don't know where to start," I continued, reaching for the croissants just as Ellie sat down. They were still warm from the oven. Bliss!

"Hashtag intrigued. Start with, what did the police have to say? And also have you called your Dad? He'll be going spare if you haven't."

"No, I haven't rung him yet. I haven't had time."

She sighed loudly. "Why don't you ring him now then? While I eat croissants?"

I rolled my eyes but did as Ellie had suggested. He barely said two words to me before handing the phone to my Mum.

"He's not really speaking to me at the minute," I filled Ellie in after disconnecting. "He's still mad because I fell asleep and forgot to text last night."

"He's just worried about you, Emma. He's not really angry."

"Oh he is. He said as much. He said that if I couldn't be bothered to send one teeny tiny text message to save him a night's worth of worry, then he couldn't be bothered speaking to me on the phone." Two words had actually been nearer to thirty.

Ellie snickered. "He'll get over it, it's only because he's worried. What did the police have to say then?"

"I haven't rung them yet either and before you rag on at me…" I got in there before she could tell me off, "…I've only just gotten up. I was about to ring them when you arrived. And now there are croissants to eat."

"You were up ages ago, you texted me remember?"

"Well, yes. But I had to get showered and dressed first. And it takes more than five minutes to look this good you know." I tossed my head and bit into my own croissant, now liberally filled with jam. "Mmm, this is good," I mumbled with a mouth full, crumbs dropping everywhere.

What's that? Blake asked, again in the depths of my mind.

Stop that, I snapped, without even thinking about whether or not it was possible for me to converse with Blake telepathically. It was very disconcerting having him talking to me in the silence of my mind while I was trying to have a conversation with Ellie.

But what is it? Blake asked again. *I can taste something sweet.*

You can taste what I'm eating now? I asked. *Oh for fucks sake,* I cursed silently. I genuinely didn't swear all that much and especially not around my parents, but in what was supposed to be the sanctuary of my own mind I figured I could say what I liked. The only positive that I could take from his answer was that this communication channel was not one sided at least.

"Consider yourself told off. You promised you would call the police," Ellie continued a little sternly bringing me back to the actual conversation I was having.

"And I will, straight after breakfast," I reassured. "You can even listen into my call now."

"There is that," she answered.

"No jam?" I asked, changing the subject. She was eating her croissant neat.

"They don't need jam. They're so fresh. Anyway, what did you want to tell me if it wasn't what the police said? You haven't had another letter have you?"

"No, nothing like that." I took a deep breath and plunged into my news. "This is going to sound crazy, it's about Mr. TDH. I've learned so much about him. He's the Grim Reaper and he's my soulmate." There I'd said it.

"Uh-huh, that was last night's dream, was it? Talk about a leap, from some guy standing in the corner of your bedroom to him being the Grim Reaper. Usually I'm the one with the vivid imagination."

"No Ellie, it wasn't a dream. His name's Blake and he's the Grim Reaper. Eons ago the original Grim Reaper gave up his soul so that his lover could have a child. I've got that soul. Well, a part of it anyway, Blake has the other part of it."

"You were born eons ago?"

"No, silly. The soul has been passed down through the generations to me."

"Emma," Ellie put down the croissant that she was eating and reached over to hold my hand. "You're not making any sense and this doesn't just sound crazy, it is crazy."

"I know, I'm not explaining it very well, am I?"

"Honey, I know you haven't been sleeping very well recently but the supernatural doesn't exist, so whatever you think you've learned, it was just a dream. Fairy tales, goblins, Grim Reapers, they're not real."

"It's the Keeper of Souls," Blake shouted from upstairs, irritated.

"Who said that?" Ellie asked, looking around.

"It was Blake. I told you, he wasn't just a dream. I mean, I was dreaming about him but he does exist." I raised my voice, "Blake, please come downstairs."

Ellie looked puzzled, "Emma, I don't understand what's going on? Is that your brother? Is he hiding up there to play a joke on me? Now is not the time for tricks, not with everything that is going on."

"No, I promise. I would never do that to you."

"Well, is it the guy that's been stalking you? Have you got Stockholm Syndrome?"

"No, I haven't got Stockholm Syndrome. I don't think it's even possible to get that unless you've been held captive. Blake!" I raised my voice again frustrated that Blake hadn't helped me out, "Get down here. You can try the jam for yourself," I bargained, hoping that would be enough to persuade him.

Blake's intrigue got the better of him and I heard him on the stairs. "Where's the jam?" he asked. He'd spent centuries as a voyeur, never being able to touch or feel anything, never being able to experience the world around him. His desire for everything was overwhelming. His longing pulsed inside of me. He wanted to touch everything, feel everything, do everything and especially taste the jam.

"Blake, this is Ellie," I said gesturing to her. "And Ellie, this is Blake. I told you he was real." I handed Blake the jar of jam. Having felt the depth of his desire I didn't want to stand between him and his first taste.

Various emotions flickered across Ellie's face. She was clearly concerned and confused. "It's nice to meet you," she said to Blake before turning to me. "Emma, what are you doing letting strangers into your house, especially right now?" she hissed. "Whoever this guy is, whatever he's told you, he's not the Grim Reaper. I can't believe you've fallen for this. You! You're the sceptical one," she paused before turning to Blake and adding politely, "I'm sorry."

"Again, it's the Keeper of Souls," Blake answered distractedly, barely glancing at Ellie. He hadn't bothered with a spoon but had instead dipped a finger into the jam and was busy testing how it felt between his finger and thumb. "It's tacky," he said, more to himself than to anyone else it seemed.

"Try it," I urged. "And then will you go and sit on the bench at the bottom of the garden. I'm hoping that will be enough to prove to Ellie that you're who you say you are."

Blake didn't answer, lost in his jar of jam, but somewhat

surprisingly he did do as I'd asked without any argument, leaving sticky handprints on the back door as he went.

"Emma, stop this," Ellie said. "I'm getting worried about you." She pleaded at me with her whole body, her face drawn and pinched, her eyes clouded with worry.

"Just watch him walk away, please," I begged.

Ellie sighed sadly, perhaps mentally preparing to check me into a psych ward, but she did turn in her seat and dutifully watch as Blake walked towards the bench. I felt it when he stepped beyond my reach, the strange pop as moved beyond from my sphere of influence. Ellie gasped. I could still see Blake very clearly. To me it just looked like he walked so far, dropped the jar of jam and then turned back to glare at me, albeit he did stay put. But to Ellie he simply disappeared. She watched him blink out of existence and the jar of jam fall to the ground where it hit the grass with a thud and then rolled away from Blake.

"What the…" she started to say, half rising in her seat. "Where did he go? What just happened?" She turned back to me, confusion written all over her face.

"I told you. He's the Grim Reaper. He's my soulmate. Proximity to me forces him to manifest but when he moves too far away from me he reverts back to being a spirit. I can still see him because of our connection but you can't. You can only see him when he's close to me."

"He's the…" Ellie paused, she looked extremely shaken. "Emma, this isn't possible. The Grim Reaper doesn't exist, he's a myth. There must be another explanation for all of this."

"For the fact that you just saw a man disappear with your own eyes?" I asked as gently as I could but even I heard the edge in my voice. Ellie's disbelief had hurt me and a small vicious part of me — a part that I mostly tried to ignore — felt victorious in her suffering. "What other explanation is there?"

Ellie didn't answer, she had a lot of processing to do.

I thought she'd understand, I directed my thoughts at Blake, unsure if he would be able to hear them or not.

I can always hear you.

But I thought…? I left it hanging.

A correction then. From close by I can always hear you.

Oh, I replied. *Why doesn't she believe me?* I asked angrily.

Why does it matter if she believes you or not? Blake's tone was dispassionate, uncaring almost.

Because she's my best friend. I found it odd that Blake had to ask. *She's my Seith,* I added by way of explanation. A very faint ripple of understanding and compassion mixed with a significant amount of confusion washed over me. Blake had spent centuries with people but he didn't fully comprehend their complexities.

He offered an explanation anyway, presumably because of the tiny amount of sympathy he'd felt. *You've been dreaming about me for months. You've seen me with my weapon. You've shared a vision with me. And you have a part of my soul. This is your destiny, not hers.*

"Ellie, do you want anything?" I asked, feeling guilty for my earlier anger.

"I don't... this isn't possible. There must be another explanation. Maybe he's just hiding?"

"He's not hiding, Ellie." I reached across the table and hugged her into me despite the edge of the table that cut into my stomach. "I know this is unbelievable. But I need you to believe it, to believe me."

"But, if he's the Grim Reaper…"

Keeper of Souls, Blake interjected.

"…shouldn't he be out there, reaping souls?"

I am.

You are?

Of course. It's my purpose.

"He is. He says he is anyway," I answered Ellie. "Blake, why don't you come back in now?"

He chose to materialise in the lounge and, while it caused Ellie to jump, I was getting more blasé after my earlier bathroom experience. The bigger surprise to me was that his fingers were clean again. Turning incorporeal seemed to reset him somehow.

"Didn't you bring the jam back inside?" I asked.

"It rolled away from me when it fell," he replied before addressing Ellie. "Ellie," he inclining his head in a formal greeting. "You have questions," he asked politely, although I sensed he had no real desire to engage with Ellie. The world around him he seemed interested in but people, not so much.

Me and Ellie turned properly in our seats to face Blake. "I do," she said quite firmly. "I want to know how you're performing these tricks because this cannot be real. I mean, if it is, shouldn't you be ferrying people to the other side?"

"I am." Blake sounded indignant again, he clearly didn't like being questioned. "Right now three people are taking their last breaths and I am with them all. 18 more will follow in the next few seconds and hundreds more in the next few hours. I will be with them all. I don't know how I do what I do but I am where I need to be when I need to be. And I am also here, my consciousness is here. The…" Blake searched for the right word, "…copies of me are not conscious in their own right but I can feel them all. They're a part of me."

"That doesn't even begin to make sense," Ellie said. But to me it sort of did. I didn't fully understand it but I felt like I was on the verge of getting it. Maybe because it was my destiny and not hers.

"Ellie, are you okay?" I asked.

"My head hurts," she replied. "This, on top of everything else. It's just too much."

"Do you want to go?" I asked softly. "I understand if you do." I couldn't keep the sadness out of my voice because I was desperate for Ellie to be a part of whatever the future held for me.

"I do," she replied and my heart sank. Ellie had been with me through everything. She'd always been there for me, even when I perhaps hadn't deserved it. The thought of losing her was unbearable. "But I'm not going anywhere," she concluded straightening her spine. "I said I'd be there for you no matter what and I will be. I can't promise to understand what's going on here and I still think there could be another explanation but I'm not going anywhere. Now then," she declared, "pass me the chocolate spread. I think I'm going to need it!"

I sighed the biggest sigh of relief that it was possible to sigh and squeezed Ellie's hand before turning to Blake. "There is one thing that I don't understand," I said, "you keep saying that you're the one who reaps people's souls when they die but you don't, do you? The…" I paused trying to remember Blake's word.

Copies, he supplied in the silence of my mind.

"…copies actually do the doing. So, what's your role in all of this?"

"I am the Keeper of Souls," Blake declared as though that answered my question.

"So you've said," I replied with only a hint of sarcasm.

"Are you like the Multiple Man from the X-Men movies?" Ellie asked, earning a look from Blake. It was evident that she was still confused, but she didn't seem to be afraid. Neither was I actually, which wasn't rational, but none of what was happening made logical sense.

"You mean the guy who can duplicate himself? How do you even know what his name is?" I asked.

Ellie turned a shade of pink but didn't answer, she just nodded and looked expectantly at Blake.

"I don't know what else to tell you," Blake shrugged. "I am the Keeper of Souls, I absorb the souls of the dying. If four people from across the world die at the same time, I'll be with them all. I am the copies, I think."

"What do you mean, you think?" I asked.

"Being the Keeper of Souls didn't exactly come with a manual," Blake bit back.

This line of questioning wasn't getting us anywhere, so I asked something else that had been bothering me: "How come Cooper and Watson seem so relaxed with you?"

"That's obvious," Ellie answered before Blake could even open his mouth. She certainly seemed to have started accepting Blake for what he was. "Animals don't worry about Death like we do."

"I am not Death," Blake stated. His annoyance filtered into my consciousness. Without realising it I had been feeling all of his emotions as well as my own. I settled back into my seat, choosing to let Ellie and Blake argue this one out between themselves, choosing to watch their interaction instead of trying to mediate the argument that was brewing.

"You know what I mean," Ellie dismissed.

"I do not," Blake shot back. "I am not Death. I am the Keeper of Souls, I do not cause anyone's demise."

"You could though if you wanted to, couldn't you?"

I tuned out their conversation and focused on what I was feeling, a huge sense of relief mixed with a reasonably large dollop of amusement. Ellie was my very best friend and Blake was my… well, I didn't really know what he was to me. It felt too soon to use the term 'boyfriend' and I couldn't really call him my soulmate, even if the latter was factually correct, so what was he to me? Whatever he was, it was entertaining watching the two of them spar.

Blake, on the other hand, was a welter of confused emotions. He was disorientated by what was happening to him, delighted and irritated all at the same time. From what I'd seen he had no real interest in people (with the possible exception of me) however, he was enjoying being in a conversation. Perhaps because it was a new experience for him. He hated being questioned though, I felt a spike of irritation every time Ellie argued against him. And because we were reflecting each other's emotions he was struggling with what I was feeling. Poor Blake. He had a lot to learn about being human.

If only I hadn't been so engrossed in sorting through our different emotions, I might have identified who my stalker was.

CHAPTER 15 – EMMA

Monday 11th February 2019

No-one was sure when it had been delivered but there it was, a second letter, in exactly the same type of expensive-looking, cream-coloured envelope as the first one. The envelope even had the same four words written in block capitals on its front: For Miss Emma Moore. Almost as though it had been foretold by Ellie.

"How did none of us see this being delivered?" I gestured at the letter, which now lay on the dining room table. I was so cross with myself, I'd missed my chance to catch whoever was stalking me in the act. My anxiety levels had crept up a notch but I was pleasantly surprised by the fact that they'd only crept up a notch. Although what was keeping me sane I didn't know: Blake's presence, Ellie's presence, a good night's sleep or plain old acceptance. Whatever it was, I was grateful for it.

"We were busy," Ellie answered. "There were croissants to eat and questions to be asked and then we had to clean up." She and I were both seated at the dining room table again, much as we had been during breakfast. "If we hadn't tidied up, we'd still be none the wiser," she pointed out. We'd only found the letter because we'd put the Tupperware that Ellie's Mum had packed the croissants into at the front door, ready for when Ellie left.

"Blake, didn't you see *anything*?" I asked. His interest in the letter had been minimal. It was nothing more than an inconvenience to him, a distraction from the pleasures of being corporeal. He stood at the fridge, its door wide open, sampling various foodstuffs. So far, cheese had gone down well, as had yoghurt.

"Nothing," he answered. He had the jar of garlic in his hand.

"I wouldn't if I were you," I advised. "It doesn't taste all that nice on its own."

Blake ignored me and unscrewed the cap.

"You won't like it," I reiterated.

"I might. You've experienced all that life has to offer whereas I've had to watch from the side-lines. I've been denied everything, unable to do anything more than watch as life passed me by. I want to try it."

"Fine, be my guest." There was a dry edge to my voice.

Me and Ellie both watched as he sampled. And then we both laughed out loud at his obvious displeasure. We got scowled at in return but it had been worth it.

Ellie sobered up first and asked, "So, are you going to open it?"

"Do you think I should?"

"You might as well. Then you can tell the police what both letters say. Because that's next on the to-do list."

"Okay." I sighed but reached for the envelope.

My dearest Emma, the love of my life,

It was wonderful seeing you at yesterday's open day, so relaxed and happy. I am glad that I was a part of it, able to spend time with you that I otherwise wouldn't have gotten.
Valentine's Day is fast approaching. I have a surprise for you, one that I hope you'll like even more than the bouquet of roses. You deserve a little spoiling, you give so much of yourself to others and to the care of the animals, it's time someone did something extravagant for you.

Forever and always xx

"Creepy," I concluded giving the letter to Ellie so that she could also read it.

"Indeed," Ellie agreed, having swiftly read the letter. "I wonder what surprise he has planned for you. That's a little scary."

"Or she," I argued.

"Emma, it's not Charlotte," Ellie replied adamantly.

"How can you be so sure? There's nothing in that letter that rules her out and evidently it's someone who was at the open day."

"The syntax suggests it wasn't a staff member though. Plenty of people were at the open day. Where's the first letter, maybe there are some clues in there?"

"I don't think so," I answered dubiously while I dutifully retrieved the first letter from where I'd stashed it and handed it to Ellie.

"Ah ha!" She declared. "Right here, proof that it's no-one we work with. 'It was nice of you to take them into the care home, who do you visit there?' He's talking about Grammy. Everyone at work knows about Grammy."

"Everyone? Matthew and Charlotte included. They've only worked with us for three months. I don't think I've ever talked about her to them."

"We must have done. I must have done! Grammy must have come up in conversation even if it was only because of the what-have-you-been-up-to-this-weekend question."

"I honestly don't know. I might have mentioned her but I'm not sure."

"What are you two talking about?" Blake interrupted.

"Tried everything in the fridge, have you?"

"Yes."

"You do know that I'm being stalked, don't you? I thought you might have shown a little more interest." My temper flared suddenly at his disinterest.

"What does it matter if you're being stalked?"

"It's not a nice thing, you know? To have someone watching you all the time, following you wherever you go. And what if I get hurt, or killed?" I suggested the possibility that I might get murdered only to provoke some kind of reaction from Blake but, as the words left my mouth, a ripple of fear ran through me. What if I was hurt as a result of being stalked? It seemed unlikely. Surely you wouldn't hurt the love of your life, which was how I'd been addressed in both of the letters. But stalkers were crazy, weren't they? On television they were anyway. Were real life stalkers as dangerous as the ones on television? Was my initial panic warranted? Or was it just a nuisance?

"I watch people. I follow people." Blake interrupted before I could get too lost in my internal dialogue. He must have felt my fear but if he had he didn't respond to it, perhaps because Ellie was there or perhaps because he didn't care. Who knew with Blake.

"That's different."

"How's it different? Besides, you're in no danger of dying any time soon."

"How can you be so sure? Do you know when I am going to die?"

"No, I just know that you aren't going to die any time soon."

"How do you know that for a fact?"

Blake huffed impatiently. "I can sense death in a person's future. You have none."

That was new. And interesting. "You can see into the future?" Ellie asked.

"No, I didn't say that."

"You did," I quickly sided with Ellie. "How far into the future can you see?"

"I can't see into the future," Blake was obviously irritated. "But I can sense the likelihood of someone dying," he added. And then, with a top note of pride, he volunteered additional information "and if I focus I can see how the different probabilities manifest themselves."

"Wow! That's so cool. How long before the probabilities resolve themselves?" I persisted.

"I've never timed it. I've never needed to. Sometimes minutes, sometimes days."

"How does it work?"

"I don't know, I've never had to explain it before."

"Try," I coaxed.

Blake sighed loudly before explaining. Pride crept into his voice again though. "When someone is faced with a choice that may result in their death or when their time draws to a close, I can feel it. I am drawn to it. In the case of a choice I can weigh up the options and when I concentrate I can 'see' the resultant outcome of each one."

"Cool," I murmured. Although it could easily have been Ellie, we were both fascinated, transfixed by Blake's narrative.

Blake seemed to be willing to answer our questions for the moment and so we peppered him with them.

"What sort of choices?"

"What do you mean by see?"

Blake chose to answer my question first. "In my mind, like when I bear witness to someone's life as I reap their soul."

"You…?" I started to ask but Blake was already answering Ellie's question. His pride had got the better of him and he was actually enjoying himself. In a way, he was showing off. In another place and at another time, I might have called it conceited but I could actually feel his pleasure. He couldn't help but be delighted by the interest we were showing in him.

"All sorts of choices, to turn left or to turn right, to eat the chicken or the beef, to stay home for the day or to go out."

"Such simple things," Ellie breathed. She was hanging onto

Blake's every word. Mind you, so was I. It wasn't every day that you got to hang out with the stuff of myth and legend.

"What else can you do?" It was my turn again.

"Whatever I need to do. Go anywhere. Be everywhere."

"You can go anywhere?" Ellie asked. "Have you been to the North Pole?"

Blake nodded.

"What about China?"

Blake nodded again.

"What about…"

"Yes. I've been there too." Blake answered before Ellie could finish her question. "There is nowhere I haven't been. Nothing I haven't seen."

"Were you on the Titanic?" I randomly choose a tragedy from the past that I was familiar with.

"Yes," Blake answered without elaborating.

"How old are you?" Ellie ventured into the territory of personal details. I winced, assuming Blake would not answer but to my surprise he seemed non-plussed.

"My memories start in the year 1027."

"1027," Ellie repeated. "That would make you… what? Nine hundred and something?"

"Nine hundred and ninety two depending on when he was actually born." I answered on behalf of Blake, he'd mentioned the year previously and I'd idly done the maths. Since then I'd been trying hard not to think too much about the fact that he was nearly a thousand years old and I wasn't even thirty.

"What a life you must have had," Ellie was still enrapt.

Blake didn't respond. I couldn't hear his thoughts in the same way that he could hear mine so I didn't know what it was about that statement that made him lose interest in the conversation but his emotions changed rapidly. He'd been enjoying being the centre of attention but then, all of a sudden, his enthusiasm for it dimmed and a wave of sadness washed over him.

"Goodness! Is that the time?" I exclaimed in mock surprise, making a point of looking exaggeratedly at the clock I kept on the kitchen wall. "Blimey, you'd best be off." I stood and gently pushed Blake, encouraging him to leave. I didn't know what it was that had caused his mood to change, but sympathy had welled up inside of me and I suddenly wanted nothing more than to spare him from any more questions.

"What time is it?" Ellie asked looking at her own watch. If I'd appeared false in any way, she didn't pull me on it. "Wow, it's nearly two o'clock. And you still haven't rung the police."

"No, and I do need to," I answered. I was a little bit distracted though because what I was actually thinking about was whether or not I should kiss Blake goodbye. Having decided to move the conversation on, and to let him leave for some respite, the thought had occurred that I didn't know the appropriate way to say goodbye. One thought had then led to another. It seemed a little too soon to be making out with him in front of my best friend but I did want to kiss him. And to have him kiss me back, his hands sliding up my back and into my hair.

Blake solved the problem for me. *Later,* he all but growled in my mind. "I'II leave you both then," he announced out loud. And with that he disappeared from the lounge, leaving my sphere of influence with that strange pop that was starting to feel almost normal.

There was no denying that me and Ellie were both stunned by some of what Blake had had to say but, despite her enthusiasm during the conversation, once he'd left Ellie resumed her search for a rational explanation. Any rational explanation.

In comparison, I realised, I'd accepted everything that he'd had to say quite readily. Ellie had been on point when she'd said I was the sceptical one, I didn't believe in anything without proof. It was strange how willingly I'd heard what Blake had had to say and how easily I'd come to accept it as the truth. Why hadn't I wanted tangible evidence? Was it because I really did share a soul with Blake? Was it my destiny? Or was my judgement impaired because of everything that had happened to me recently? And if that was the case, was my judgement impaired in all matters, was I being overconfident when it came to the issue of my stalker? Was I truly 'all right' as I had repeatedly told my Dad or was I actually in any danger as I had suggested to Blake?

"You still need to ring the police," Ellie said suddenly.

"On it," I replied reaching for my phone.

"No more delaying tactics?"

"No, no more delaying tactics. It looks like I've got an interesting life ahead of me, I want to be around to live it."

"Do you really think the stalker could become aggressive?"

"I don't know. I only suggested it to provoke some kind of reaction from Blake but now that I've said it... you did the research on stalking, what do you think?"

"I don't know either. I guess it depends on what type of stalker you've got."

"There are different kinds?"

"Oh yes. Five or six if I remember rightly, ranging from someone who has been dumped and can't, or won't, get over it to someone who stalks their victims with the intent of harming them. Don't worry, I don't think that last one applies to you," she added hastily, "I don't think those kind of stalkers buy their victims flowers or send them love letters. Have you dumped anyone recently, kicked them out of bed with their pants around their ankles?" she asked, her eyes wide with feigned innocence.

I gave Ellie 'the look'. "You know full well that I have not." Neither Ellie nor I had had any serious relationships. Relationships, yes. Serious, no. Although she wouldn't admit it, Ellie was waiting for my brother and I was... well, evidently I'd been waiting for Blake.

I dialled 1-0-1 before Ellie could ask anything else. She had a dirty mind, who knew what she'd come out with next.

"Thank-you for calling the Lancashire Constabulary. Please hold the line for one of our operators," a perky, and somewhat obviously, recorded voice said to me.

"I'm on hold," I said to Ellie. "You can go if you want. Who knows how long I'll be."

"I'll wait, I want to know what they have to say," she replied. "And I don't entirely trust you not to abandon the call on the pretence of trying later when it might be quieter," she added. "Just because you said you'd ring them... well, you know what I'm trying to say."

"What? As if I would!" I exclaimed.

In the end I only waited 20 minutes or so until a male voice at the other end of the line spoke up. "Good afternoon, thank-you for holding, my name is Will. How may I help you today?"

"Erm, hi," I answered, a little startled to have gotten through at last. "I need to report a stalker, that is, I'm being stalked. I'd like to make a report please."

"No problem, let me start by taking your name please."

"It's Emma, Emma Moore." I could hear Will typing away on his computer.

"That's great, thank-you Emma. May I call you Emma?"

"Yes, that's fine." I said. *What else would you call me?* I wondered.

"And if you could just give me your address."

I dutifully gave my address.

"And your telephone number?"

I gave my telephone number.

"And lastly your date of birth?"

I gave my date of birth.

"Okay, so what makes you think you're being stalked Emma?"

"I started seeing a dark blue sedan, I mean an SUV following me. And then I received a bouquet of roses at work. I thought maybe someone liked me but then a letter was delivered to my house. It all but says I'm being stalked. I got a second one today. A letter that is." I heard more typing.

"That's fine, thank-you," Will said as he typed. "The car you've noticed, do you have a make or model?"

"No."

"Registration number?"

"No."

"Okay, not to worry. But you're sure about the colour?"

"Yes, I am sure about that."

"And the flowers, where are they now?"

"I gave them away. I don't have them anymore."

"Do you know who they were from? Who delivered them?"

"I don't know who they're from…" *because if I did I would know who was stalking me,* I added silently, "…but they were delivered by Interflora."

"Lovely." More typing. "And the letters, what did they say?"

"I've got them here, do you want me to read them out for you?"

"Yes please, that would be helpful."

I did as instructed.

"Super. That's great, thank-you. Can I ask you to put them somewhere safe for me? We'll need those to investigate. Perhaps secure them in a plastic bag for me so that you don't handle them anymore."

"Okay." *Plastic bag, noted.*

"And is there anything else that you think I should know? Any idea who might be stalking you?"

"No, none whatsoever."

"Nooo problem," Will said while continuing to type, drawing out the 'o' in 'no' to give himself time to update the record he was creating. "Here's what we're going to do. We're going to make an appointment with a Police Constable for you. The Police Constable will take some more details and then investigate further. Let's see if we can identify this person, shall we?"

More details? I thought. "Great, thanks," I said out loud.

"Now, what would you prefer? The Police Constable can come out to you, or you can go into your local police station."

"Out to me I guess. When will it be?"

"My next available appointment is…" I heard yet more typing as he searched, "…with PC Danny Martin tomorrow morning. I can't give an exact time because there is always the possibility that he'll be called to an emergency. Is that any good to you?"

"Not really," I answered, pulling a face. "I'm due in work in the morning."

"That's not a problem, he can come to your workplace or we can find another appointment. Your choice."

I sighed. Enough people at work knew anyway, why not make it everyone? And I was fairly certain that Andrew wouldn't mind me taking a break whenever mister-PC-Danny-Martin showed up otherwise he'd face the wrath of my Dad. "Work is fine, it's Cedar's Veterinary Centre."

"Lovely, that's all booked in for you then. If you could have the letters with you to hand over as evidence that would be great. Try not to handle them anymore please. And last but not least, your incident number is LC-20190211-0239. Please quote this number if you ring us again."

"Hold on, I just need pen and paper," I said while gesticulating to Ellie, who thank-fully understood and passed me what I needed. "It was LC what?" I asked.

"LC hyphen 20190211 hyphen 0239."

"LC," I mumbled while writing down the number. "Got it, thanks."

"Perfect. Have a nice day now," Will concluded and hung up.

"Done, and done!" I said to Ellie as I hung up the phone.

"Why don't you text your Dad straight away? He'll be pleased to know that you've made an appointment with the police. It might even put you back in his good books."

"We can hope," I said while typing a quick message to both of my parents.

I've rung the police. I've got an appointment with a Police Constable tomorrow morning. They're going to try and find out who is stalking me. Xx

Fairly swiftly I received their replies, both of which summed up each of my parents perfectly.

My Mum's reply said: *Good girl. Keep working the problem. Xx*

My Dad's reply on the other hand said: *Good! What time? Where? I'll come and sit in on the appointment with you.*

"Sigh," I said to Ellie, my shoulders sagging. "My Dad now wants to come to the appointment."

"He's just worried about you. Tell him that he doesn't need to because I'll be there. Tell him he's the best for offering. He'll be happy then."

"Okay," I answered. "When did you become such an expert in managing my Dad?" I asked as I typed a reply to him.

I haven't been given an exact time, just in case there is an emergency. You don't need to sit with me though, the cop is coming to work so Ellie will be with me. Thank-you for offering though. You're the best! Xx

"Too much?" I asked, showing Ellie the text I'd written.

"You could lay it on even thicker with your Dad but then he might start to suspect something so, yes go with that."

I hit send and received a smiley face in reply.

"Wow it worked," I exclaimed.

"Told ya!" Ellie said smirking and buffing her fingernails cheekily across the top of her shirt. "Now then, tell me everything that you know about Blake, from the beginning."

Potentially it was going to be a long afternoon.

CHAPTER 16 – BLAKE

Monday 11th February 2019

Blake was stood in the centre of an American Casino, taking comfort in the normality of the situation. It was early o'clock in the morning but the casino was still busy, people played the tables, fed quarters into slot machines and wandered aimlessly about in the eternal gloom. Blake loved the big casino's, there was always something going on and, because the gambling floors were kept at a constant temperature with low levels of lighting, it was easy to lose track of time.

Despite the endless hustle and bustle no-one took any notice of him. No-one looked at him or spoke to him. No-one asked him questions. No-one wanted to know what he could do or how he could do the things that he could do. No-one even knew he was there. Blake felt at peace. He'd longed for company, never truly accepting Seith as a friend. He'd hated being alone. He'd yearned for someone — anyone — to acknowledge his presence, but he'd never realised how exhausting it was going to be when it finally happened.

He'd experienced the most eventful two days of his life. He'd met his soulmate, felt the wind, kissed a girl, touched actual objects and tasted different foodstuffs. And he'd been grilled! His emotions were in turmoil. He'd experienced joy, irritation, pride… a whole welter of emotions. Before meeting Emma it had been a long time since Blake had felt anything other than apathy. Lastly, he'd been left confused by how quickly he'd lost interest in the conversation when his life had come up. In truth, he'd been relieved to escape from that part of the conversation.

To distract himself, he scanned the casino floor sensing death.

Few in the room had any chance of dying but there were some.

An old man playing the slot machines was almost guaranteed to die. Blake watched him for a while dispassionately. He would have a heart attack when the machine he was playing on paid out. His only glimmer of hope currently lay snoring in a basement flat on the other side of the city. If, and it was a big if, the snorer slept through her alarm she wouldn't be driving a bus when she was pulled back into the land of nod. Falling asleep at the wheel wouldn't cost her her own life, but it would cost eleven others theirs, eight of whom were schoolchildren. Paramedics would be called to the scene from across the city and, as a consequence, no-one would be available to respond to the emergency call from the casino. However, if the bus driver slept through her alarm, everyone would live. But the old man had a 99% chance of dying.

A bride, or at least a woman dressed in a wedding gown bimbling around by herself because Blake had long ago learned that looks could be deceiving (especially in Las Vegas), had mixed odds. After learning the fate of the slot machine man, Blake focussed his attention on her. Ironically, she needed to drink more in order to save herself. If she drank herself into oblivion, she'd pass out before she could think that it would be fun to fly from one of the many balconies in the hotel.

Blake watched the occupants of the casino impervious to their fates. He had no real interest in people as individuals. Whether or not they lived or died was irrelevant. That was just the way of things, all people were born only to die. That was their sole purpose. He watched them because what else was there for him to do? The world was not his to be a part of; he was not able to feel the chill of snowflakes as they fell softly from the sky nor was he able to feel the warmth of the sun on his face. He could not reach out and pick up an ice-cold tin of pop nor taste its contents. Their world was not his world, he was only allowed to watch from the side-lines. Unless he was with Emma it would seem.

"Emma," he murmured to himself, thinking that maybe if he said her name out loud someone would hear him. She was his link to the world after all. But no-one did. No-one near him paused for a beat or stopped and listened, they just carried on about their business, gambling and drinking. Did he even have a voice if no-one could hear him? Was he even a being if no-one could perceive him?

The thought of Emma made Blake smile faintly. When he'd first felt her calling to him he'd been enraged at her for daring to exert her will over his. He was the Keeper of Souls after all, the only Keeper of Souls. No-one had that right. In fact, he'd long ago concluded that no-one had that sort of power. His anger had been tinged with fear. Fear and lust because Emma was beautiful. She was blessed with long copper-coloured hair, symmetrical features and a smattering of freckles that gave her a sun-kissed look even in the depths of winter. From the first moment that Blake had laid eyes on her he'd wanted her, he'd longed for her. His desire had been like nothing he'd ever experienced previously. And now that he knew who she was he wanted her even more.

An alarm rang in the casino. Blake had lost a couple of hours in thought and time had run out for the slot machine man. Blake watched as coins started to pour from the machine. The tray filled up and overflowed. Sirens rang and lights flashed. Various people congratulated the old man, clapping him on his back. He looked delighted, he literally jumped for joy. But then his delight turned to terror and he clutched at his chest. Blake continued to watch as he collapsed in pain. The atmosphere changed, people took a step backwards and called out for others to dial 9-11 as the old man struggled to catch his breath, and slowly slipped away.

Blake knew when it was over. He watched himself kneel beside the body. He watched himself lean over it and draw its soul out with the Kiss of Death. And as he reaped the soul he learned that the old man's name was Chuck, that he'd never married and that he was 61 years old, not quite as old as he'd looked. He'd lived in Las Vegas his whole life, spending thousands on the slot machines. He'd never won more than $50 but he'd continued to play telling himself that one day he'd win big. 'One day' had finally come, but the stress of it had triggered a heart attack. Blake felt Chuck's sorrow as he died, with his last breath he realised that he'd wasted his life waiting for 'one day'.

Blake shifted his consciousness and surveyed the scene of the accident that had sealed Chuck's fate, the accident that had been caused when the bus driver had fallen asleep at the wheel. From where he stood it appeared as though the bus had swerved across the highway colliding with oncoming traffic. A quirk of fate had caused it to tip over and slide a ways down the highway, propelled backwards by the traffic that ploughed into it. Noise filled the air as people screamed in pain and terror. Police cars, fire trucks and ambulances had all rushed to the scene and officials ran to help wherever possible. But it was too late for the eleven. Blake had already reaped their souls.

Blake felt nothing for the lives that had been lost. A part of living was dying. His duty, his purpose, was to reap the souls. He stood watching the scene without any sense of regret. And then he felt Emma calling out to him, pulling him to her.

Blake wanted Emma, she was his soulmate after all, his link to the world. But she had all the power, even if she wasn't aware of it, and while he delighted in being able to touch and feel and taste and smell when he was with her, he couldn't help but feel a tiny amount of resentment towards her. She enjoyed the pleasures of living every day, he could only enjoy them when he was inside her bubble (as she'd called it). Before he'd met Emma he'd been resigned to the way things were, he'd been settled after so many years of anger and anguish. Now though, he'd had a taste of how life could be. He'd experienced the wonder of living and he wanted it on his terms instead of on hers. He wanted to be able to reach out when it suited him, not just when she was near him.

He felt her calling him again, the compulsion stronger this time. He resisted for as long as he could but she compelled him and he had to respond. His life had definitely been easier before meeting Emma.

CHAPTER 17 – EMMA

Monday 11th February 2019

"Blake, are you there? Ellie's gone if you wanted to come back." I waited but he didn't magically appear in a non-existent puff of smoke. Ellie had evidently made him feel uncomfortable somehow, and so I'd naturally assumed he'd come straight back when she left. Or maybe he hadn't heard me. He had said something about only being able to hear me when he was in close proximity with me. So, maybe that was it. It was certainly the more palatable of the options.

"Blake?" I tried again, willing him to appear, concentrating on that one word so hard that I thought I'd burst, desperately wanting him with me. Nothing happened. I sighed and plonked myself down on the sofa, awash with feelings of frustration and a sense of restlessness. With nothing else to do, or rather nothing else that I wanted to do, I reached for my phone, hit the Facebook icon and spooled through my feed. In among the usual crap from my friends and family there was a news item that caught my eye.

A bus driver had fallen asleep at the wheel in North Las Vegas killing eleven others. I clicked on the link and read the article. Eight of the eleven were school children. My heart sank. How on earth could someone live with themselves after causing such an accident? I felt a huge amount of sympathy for the bus driver but why had she gotten behind the wheel if she'd been so tired? It just didn't make any sense.

The article was accompanied by a number of photographs from the scene of the accident. With a macabre sense of curiosity I idly scrolled through them, morbidly wanting to see if I could make sense of what had happened. The first photograph was a close-up showing the bus on its side with a tanker rammed into its underbelly. The second was a wide shot showing the whole scene. The bus and the tanker were in the centre of the picture forming a 'T' shape around which a number of other vehicles (mostly cars) were strewn at odd angles. A number of people could be seen in the second photograph, some of them were clearly hurt but others were just stood, frozen in time having been caught on camera. I zoomed into the picture, focussing my attention on the people, looking at each in turn. One woman in particular caught my eye. She was tall and willowy with long, blonde hair. She would have been smartly dressed in a navy blue suit with a white blouse if it hadn't been for the fact that the left sleeve of her jacket had been torn almost off. She was clutching her left arm across her body holding it tight with her right hand. Blood seeped through her fingers. It was evident that she'd been hurt in the accident. Aside from the obvious injury, she stared off into the distance, her eyes unfocused and glazed over. In a different setting she might have looked wistful or dreamy but against a backdrop of horror she looked spaced out. She didn't even seem to have realised that she was standing facing Blake. Instead she was looking straight through him, staring at something in the distance.

I sat looking at that part of the picture for quite a while before I realised what I was looking at. It was Blake. How was that even possible? I pinched the screen of my phone to see if I could zoom into the picture anymore and brought the phone right up to my face. It was definitely Blake.

What the f…, I thought, my thoughts trailing off before I could finish my sentence.

"How is this even possible?" I demanded. "Blake!" I yelled. "Get back here." A fury welled up inside of me. Blake had been there. He'd witnessed that accident, those deaths. Why hadn't he stopped it? Why hadn't he saved those children?

"Blake!" I yelled again, jumping up from the sofa.

"I am not your little pet to command," he replied, seemingly through gritted teeth after appearing in front of me. Any closer and we would literally be nose-to-nose. "I am the Keeper of Souls."

"What's the meaning of this?" I shoved the phone into his face, forcing him to take a step backwards.

"What's the meaning of what?"

"This. You were in Las Vegas."

"Yes, what's your point? I've told you repeatedly that I am where I need to be when I need to be."

"There was an accident. You were there, you could have

stopped it, you could have saved all of those people."

"What are you talking about?"

"The bus. The driver that fell asleep at the wheel. You were there, I saw you."

"Oh that," Blake replied nonchalantly.

"Yes that. How can you be so blasé about it?"

"I've told you before that I'm not the executioner. I only reap the souls of the dying."

"Well, that's a handy little get-out clause for you, isn't it?" I snapped. "Blah blah blah it's not my fault, guilt absolved."

"All people are born only to die. You need to accept that as a fact," Blake answered calmly.

"All people are born *only* to die!" I mimicked, my voice getting a little on the shrill side. "Do you even hear yourself? How could you say that?"

He shrugged. "Everyone who is born will die and I will be there to reap their souls. Death is the only thing certain in this life."

"Wow! I can't believe you just said that. What if it was me? What if I'd been the blonde in this photo?" I waved the phone under his nose again. "Then what?" Even if I'd wanted to, I couldn't have articulated what it was about that one woman that had made me so emotional. You'd have thought it would have been the children but, while I did grieve for them, there was something about the tall, willowy blonde.

Blake glanced at my phone briefly. "Then you would have lived. I didn't reap her soul today."

"She lived?" I asked, sinking down onto the sofa. I had no explanation for why it mattered to me but for some reason it did. The fact that she lived, even though others had died, was such a relief. A weight was lifted from my shoulders.

"Let me see the photograph again," Blake commanded. I gave up my phone and watched him study the picture. "This is me," he announced.

"Yes. And?"

"How is it possible that I am in a photograph when others can't see me?"

"I don't know. Maybe that's normal. Maybe people can't see you but a camera can?"

"Hmm," Blake responded handing back my phone but not sounding overly convinced by my theory.

"How is that bus driver going to live with herself?" I asked, changing the subject but not really expecting an answer. "After that? After killing eleven people?"

"She won't have to. She'll commit suicide on Thursday. Her fate has been sealed."

I gasped, "Oh Blake! How do you…" I broke off.

"I explained this to you earlier," Blake replied, and he had. Me and Ellie had spent quite some time trying to understand exactly what he'd said. It was such an alien concept though, that he could sense the likelihood of an individual's death.

I sighed. "It's just awful."

"She did cause a major accident that resulted in the death of eleven others. Surely she will be getting what she deserves."

"I didn't actually mean her specifically but no, this isn't what she deserves. It was an accident, that's all. A quirk of fate." I paused and then asked, "It was an accident, wasn't it?"

Blake inclined his head but didn't comment further.

"It's just awful," I repeated.

Blake came and sat next to me on the sofa. "Why is it awful?" he asked, his tone was gentler. Perhaps he was trying to understand. "All people die, accidents happen. Why is this particular event awful? You didn't even know any of the victims, plus those aren't the only lives that have been lost today. It wasn't the only tragedy."

"Why? What else has happened?" I asked, turning in my seat to look at Blake, that morbid sense of curiosity enveloping me again.

"Do you really want to know?"

"I really do. Tell me, tell me about everyone who has died today. We should mourn them all," I announced as though I knew exactly what that meant.

"You can't mourn them all. There are hundreds every day. Just in the last couple of seconds there has been a road traffic accident in Mumbai. Three people are dead because of it. And now a cancer patient has died in Sri Lanka. Over a hundred people die every minute."

"That many?" I was shocked at the figure.

"That many," Blake confirmed.

"But... I…" I faltered not really knowing what to say. "How do you deal with that?"

"Deal with what? It's life."

"You're so nasty," I criticised, but with no real anger in my voice, our fight done and dusted.

"Maybe," Blake answered softly, a trace of doubt unexpectedly creeping into his voice.

"I'm sorry, I didn't really mean that," I apologised quickly before lapsing into silence. There was so much that I wanted to say, so much that I wanted to ask but I sensed now was not the right time. Blake usually conducted himself with such an authoritative air that the trace of doubt I'd heard was unsettling. If he was unsure what hope was there for me?

"This is all so complicated," I concluded.

"It's complicated for me too," Blake replied, the doubt remaining in his voice.

Without thinking I leant towards him and kissed his cheek. "It will be all right," I said quietly.

Blake didn't reply, instead he turned towards me and kissed me full on the mouth, his hand quickly becoming entangled in my hair. I lost myself to the kiss, diving happily into the depths of oblivion, forgetting all about the accident in Las Vegas and the fact that over a hundred people died every minute. I felt like I was drowning while also being given the kiss of life, which was ironic bearing in mind who I was kissing.

Without knowing how or when it happened, I found myself on Blake's lap. One of his hands was safely cupping my bottom, cradling me into him, but the other was free to roam. And roam it did. As we kissed he lightly trailed his fingers down the side of my neck and across my breasts, along the plunging neckline of my t-shirt. Blake may have been an incorporeal being for most of his life but he had the hands and the body of someone used to doing huge amounts of manual labour and he knew exactly what to do with them. When he slid his hand inside of my clothing searching for something more than the neckline of my t-shirt, my body felt like it had been hit with a bolt of electricity. Blake held me steady on his lap and deepened our kiss.

A sense of urgency grew inside of me, I wanted more, I wanted to feel his naked body against mine but when I reached down to tug his shirt free from his pants Blake gently stopped me, capturing my hand with his.

"No," he said, pulling back from our kiss ever so slightly. "Let me savour every moment of my first time," he continued, his voice deeper, rougher and more hoarse than normal.

The words 'first time' played over and over in my mind and I let myself go, let Blake set the pace, let him decide exactly what we did until we both lay spent on the living room floor.

CHAPTER 18 – EMMA

Tuesday 12th February 2019

"First time?" Ellie asked again. Evidently I was not 'using my words' as my mother would say.

"Incorporeal being, remember? Who else could he have done it with?" I'd only reached that conclusion this morning but I sounded matronly and assured. Like the font of all knowledge.

"Well, yeah but... first time! Wow! And 'it', really? How old are you now? Was he good?" Ellie didn't pause for breath as she flitted between conversational threads.

"Ellie!" I exclaimed.

"What?" she asked, feigning innocence, her expression suitably schooled. Not that that worked on me, I'd known her for far too long. "I'd tell you," she muttered, changing her look from little-girl-lost to sulky-little-sister-slash-best-friend in the blink of an eye.

I laughed. "It was amazing, the best ever," I found myself saying despite intending to keep what had happened between Blake and myself private. Apparently wide-eyed innocence didn't work on me but I was susceptible to a good old fashioned guilt trip. Good to know!

"Ooh tell me more," Ellie answered gleefully, but before I could answer I was summoned, saved by the bell, or in this case the fatherly vet who was also my boss.

"Emma!" Andrew shouted from the reception area of Cedar's Veterinary Centre.

"Yes?" I poked my head around the corner (me and Ellie had only been in the corridor that ran from the back of the reception area behind the treatment rooms) and saw a policeman standing there.

"For you," Andrew introduced.

"Emma Moore?" the policeman asked.

"Yes, that's me," I answered as a tidal wave of guilt swept over me. I desperately tried to work out what it was that I'd done.

"We have an appointment, I'm PC Danny Martin."

I smiled, in response and in relief. Why is our natural reaction one of panic when we come face-to-face with a law enforcement officer? "Hi, yes we do. Shall we go around the back?" I asked. "Andrew, is that okay?" I sought permission.

"Use my office," Andrew replied, offering up his only personal room in the building. While no-one was exactly forbidden from using the little room at the top of the stairs, everyone understood that Andrew valued that space as his own private sanctuary. Even though I'd been at the practice for about seven years, I'd rarely set foot inside it.

Because it would have been churlish to refuse Andrew's offer I led Police Constable Danny Martin through the break room, which had the comfortable armchairs in it, and up the stairs.

Andrew's office was no bigger than my spare bedroom. However, he'd squeezed a full-sized oak desk complete with aging desk chair and a reasonably large easy chair in there. Neither of them looked inviting. The desk chair had long since mounded itself to Andrew's seated position, and the easy chair was so overstuffed that it looked like it would engulf anyone who dared sit upon it. Behind the easy chair there was a standard lamp and a bookcase. Every square inch of the place was piled high with paperwork. Luckily the practice didn't thrive because of Andrew's admin skills, it thrived because of his genuine compassion for the animals he treated. And because Andrew had been smart enough to hire a business manager who worked out of a completely separate room.

"Erm, I'll just make some space," I gestured at the mess and quickly cleared both the desk chair and the easy chair, stacking the papers on the floor because there was nowhere else for them. The policeman didn't offer to help but as soon as I'd cleared the desk chair he staked his claim. I was left to perch on the edge of the easy chair, fearful that if I sat back I was never going to stand up again. Neither chair was a great option though.

"Emma," Police Constable Danny Martin said by way of opening the conversation. "May I call you Emma?" he asked, opening a notebook that must have been in his pocket at a blank page. I inclined my head but didn't have time to answer properly before he continued, "and you must call me Danny," he insisted.

"Okay, hi," I replied unsure what else to say. It wasn't every day that you got interviewed by the police.

"So, you think you're being stalked, do you?" Danny certainly wasn't suffering from any kind of stage fright.

"I am being stalked," I answered indignantly. Danny's insinuation that I may be lying or perhaps living in a self-induced fantasy world had immediately banished any residual deference that I might have had. Danny might have been a man of the law but I wasn't going to have anyone imply that I was making stuff up.

"Of course," Danny responded, as if by rote. "But I do have to consider all the possibilities."

"What possibilities?" I asked, taking a deep breath so that the words didn't come out through clenched teeth. "There's no other explanation for what's happening to me," I concluded firmly.

"You'd be surprised," Danny answered sadly, a degree of emotion creeping into his voice for the first time. He looked up from his notebook and focussed all of his attention on me for the first time since our introduction. Danny was neither a tall man nor a fat man but he had an enormous sense of presence. He had the most penetrating stare I'd ever encountered, it was impossible to look away from his dark brown eyes. There was evidently a story there and I wondered what it was. My irritation waned and I found myself nodding absently.

"Okay," Danny replied, no doubt accepting my nod as a sign of acceptance on my behalf. His policeman mask was firmly back in place and all traces of his own personal sorrow had been banished. His slip had been so momentary that I wondered if the glimpse I'd seen was genuine or if it was an act intended to throw me off guard.

"Let's assume you're being stalked," Danny continued. "If you want me to find out who it is, I need to ask you some questions."

"Can you?" I asked. "Find who's stalking me that is." It wasn't that I didn't trust the police, in fact I had a great deal of respect for the men and women who chose to serve on the force, but there wasn't a great deal to go on.

"Honestly," Danny answered, "I don't know. Most stalkers are known to their victims and we can usually identity those ones pretty quickly, but it depends on how much the victim is willing to tell us." Danny paused, clearly wanting me to hear what he has just said. "My advice is that if you really do want my help, you'll tell me everything," he concluded.

"But I don't know anything and I definitely don't know who it is. I only have a small circle of family and friends. None of them would do anything like this."

"Are you sure about that?" Danny asked, focussing his attention on me once more.

"Absolutely," I answered, thinking only of my immediate family and Ellie.

"Think about everyone you know: people you've met here, staff and clients, old flames, people you've not spoken to in a while," Danny prompted, although how he knew that I had automatically narrowed my thinking was beyond me.

Idly I thought about everyone I knew: my parents, my brother, Ellie and her family, the practice staff... Charlotte's image arose unbidden in my mind's eye.

"Who is it?" Danny asked.

"No-one," I answered automatically. "It's not, I mean..." I faltered.

"If you suspect someone you need to tell me. If you're wrong it doesn't matter but if you're right..." Danny didn't finish but I understood what he was trying to tell me.

I sighed, my whole body drooping. "It's one of the staff here, Charlotte Wilson. Ellie thinks I'm wrong but I can't shake the feeling that it's her."

Danny made some notes in his notebook before asking, "And who's Ellie?"

"She's my best friend. I've known her forever. It's definitely not her."

"Uh-huh, not Ellie," Danny commented while writing something else in his notebook. A wry smile briefly crossed his face and I wondered again what his story was, convinced that there was one there.

"It's definitely not her. She wouldn't, and besides she has a cast-iron alibi, she was with me when both of the letters were delivered," I declared, stealing my language from the many, many crime shows that I'd watched over the years.

"Ah yes, the letters." Danny flipped to an earlier page in his notebook and read some notes he'd made previously. "I tell you what," he announced, suddenly looking up, "why don't we start at the beginning?"

"The beginning?" I asked, caught off-guard by Danny's sudden change of direction.

"Yes, why don't you tell me what happened first? What led you to believe you were being stalked?"

I paused thinking back. I'd been through this so many times recently: with Ellie, the other day at the practice, when I first contacted the police. It should have been easy to know where to start but sat there, actually with a policeman, it felt really difficult.

"At first, I didn't know that I was being stalked," I began cautiously. I wanted to tell my story logically, and I needed to ensure that nothing of Blake crept in there. "I started seeing a dark blue car behind me on a regular basis, but I wasn't sleeping well and I was tired so I assumed it was just a coincidence." I half expected Danny to jump in and ask why I hadn't been sleeping well, but he didn't. "And then I received a bouquet of roses here at work. Even then though, I wasn't sure that I was being stalked. I thought maybe I was, but I kept telling myself it wasn't possible. Why would anyone stalk me? I'm not rich, I'm not famous, I'm not anybody. It's just so bizarre. Even now I don't understand it." I stopped, contemplating that part of the puzzle further. There was nothing unusual about me apart from the fact that I was soulmates with the grim reaper. Not that I'd found that out until recently so surely no-one else knew about it, or did they? Was it possible that my stalker knew about my grim reaper heritage? Did he, or she, think that I had some kind of power? Of course, they were sadly mistaken if that was the case. And, on reflection the tone of the letters was more suitor-like than power-hungry-crazy-like. But maybe there was something there.

"But you do believe you're being stalked now?" Danny asked, prompting me to get on with it.

"Yes. Ever since I received the first letter I've been sure."

"The letters are unusual," Danny commented. "Have you brought them with you?"

"They're in my bag downstairs. I'll get them for you now if you want," I said, wondering how much effort it would take to haul myself out of the 'easy' chair, which was slowly drawing me into it. Engulfed by a chair, that would make for a novel listing on a death certificate.

"No, it's okay. I'll take them from you when we're done here. Has anything else happened since you contacted the call centre?" Danny asked.

"No, nothing connected to the stalking," I answered without thinking.

Danny raised a questioning eyebrow.

"It's erm… I… never mind." I blushed what I could only imagine was the deepest shade of pink ever to be seen in the history of mankind and sank deeper into the chair. I was never getting out of it now!

"Could he, or she, be the stalker?" Danny asked mildly, clearly connecting the dots that I had not spoken about.

"No. Absolutely not," I replied quite firmly. How could I explain who Blake was, let alone the fact that as an incorporeal being he was not capable of being my stalker?

"I see," Danny stated, again very mildly although who he assumed my rendezvous had been with escaped me.

"So, have you got everything you need?" I asked.

"I've just one or two questions," Danny answered. And so began the cross examination of my life. I thought that my Dad had been thorough but he'd barely scratched the surface compared to Danny. There was nothing he didn't want to know: each time I'd seen the car, where I'd been, if I'd been on a motorway or an A-road, if I'd seen the driver of the other car, any impressions I might have formed, when the flowers had arrived, who'd signed for them, what I'd thought about them, what I'd done with them, when the letters had arrived, what I'd been doing when they were delivered, my thoughts on the linguist style. Danny's questions were endless until he'd uncovered every little detail. And then he started asking again about my family and friends.

"What's your relationship like with your family?"

"My family?" I asked, puzzled by the line of questioning. "It's fine, why?"

"You'd be surprised at how often a stalker turns out to be a member of the victim's family."

"Well, that isn't the case here. My Dad's overprotective but he's not stalking me. I have a great relationship with my Mum and my brother is just a normal big brother."

"Grandparents? Aunts, uncles, cousins?" Danny prompted.

Mentally I rolled my eyes, my family was so not stalking me, but I answered the question all the same. And as patiently as I could. "All of my grandparents are dead. My Mum has a sister, my Aunt Catherine. She's long since divorced and I don't see her ex-husband anymore. She has twin boys, Jake and Joseph. And my Dad has two brothers, Ben is married with three children but Sam is a bit of a recluse. I don't see that much of my Dad's side of the family but there's never been a falling out, not that I know of anyway and certainly not involving me."

"Anyone else?"

"No, not in the truest sense of the word. But me and Ellie are like sisters. Her family is an extension of my own."

Danny raised a questioning eyebrow and I continued

unprompted. "Our families have always been close, me and Ellie grew up together, we went to school and university together."

"And now you work together?" Danny asked. I could hear the scepticism in his voice.

"And now we work together," I confirmed. It wasn't like the question hadn't been asked before. "Ellie's Dad knew Andrew, Andrew was hiring just after we left university and here we are. It probably sounds a bit boring to you."

"Not at all," Danny answered, fully professional once more. "And who are Ellie's parents?"

"Frank and Joanne Stephens."

"And?"

"And what? They're nice people. Joanne and my Mum went to school together. They've been best friends ever since they met. There isn't anything else to tell."

"Does Ellie have any siblings?"

"No. She's an only one."

"Does she have any other family?"

"Not living, not that I've met anyway. Well, there is Grammy but you can cross her right off your suspect list. She's 91 and in care. She's suffering with dementia. Some days are better than others but mostly she doesn't even know who we all are now. She's who we took the flowers to."

"Ah yes, you did mention her," Danny answered. "What about friends? Anyone outside of your extended family?"

"Not really. Not that I see on a regular basis anyway." My life suddenly sounded very dull to my own ears and I found myself expanding without being asked to. "I mean, I do have other friends but mostly they're Facebook friends rather than actual friends."

"I saw that you were on Facebook."

"Isn't everybody?" I shrugged.

"So it would seem," Danny replied flatly. "What about people who work here? I'll need a full list of personnel."

"There's only ten of us. Andrew owns the place, he's…" I was going to continue but Danny interrupted.

"I met him downstairs."

"Yes you did." I smiled briefly imagining what Danny might have thought of Andrew. Andrew's heart and soul belonged to his veterinary centre and the animals he cared for. He was incredibly mild mannered but people often thought him abrupt. He was kind but considered in his approach, speaking his mind only when he was decided on something. The problem some people had with Andrew was that when he had decided on something, there was no changing his mind. And he used his words sparingly, he didn't wax lyrical or soften the blow, instead he was honest and to the point, never raising his voice but never wasting time on pleasantries.

"He's lovely. All the staff are. Rhona is our receptionist, she's the practice Mum. And then there's Gary, the business manager. Angela, Matthew and Charlotte are the vets, and Tori and Noel are the other two nurses." I mentally ticked off each staff member as I named them. "The only newbies are Matthew and Charlotte."

"When did they start?"

"About November last year."

"And the stalking started…?"

"About January this year. That's partly why I wonder if it's Charlotte."

"But you don't think it could be Matthew?"

"No, not at all. He's so personable, everyone loves Matthew."

"It's easy for some people to hide who they really are, you know?"

"Yes, but why would he stalk me?"

"Why would Charlotte?"

I sighed. "Why would anyone stalk me?"

Danny didn't answer that. Instead he leafed through his notebook and then declared us done.

"What happens next?" I asked.

"Next I investigate. I'll give you a ring in two or three days with a progress report."

"And if you do find who it is? What then?"

"That's up to you. If you want we can deal with the situation informally. In many cases that solves the problem. But if you'd prefer we can issue a formal warning. Let's not get ahead of ourselves though, let me investigate and come back to you."

CHAPTER 19 – EMMA

Tuesday 12th February 2019

The smell of frying onions was making my mouth water, it was time. To the wok I added some diced chicken, some sliced peppers and onions, a lot of garlic and a sprinkle of mixed herbs. Blake had questioned the necessity of the garlic and still looked unsure but, everything I cooked contained garlic, he needed to get over his dislike. And I had told him not to try it neat.

I was a long way from being a chef — I found squeezy garlic and dried herbs much easier to work with than the fresh ingredients — but I did enjoy cooking and I'd decided during the day that Blake deserved an actual meal. Short of sampling various food stuffs from my kitchen cupboards he'd never eaten anything and that was something I sympathised with.

When the chicken was mostly browned, I added a stock cube and some water to my creation demonstrating again just how far away I was from being a chef. I'm sure a true chef would have made the stock rather than just adding the separate ingredients to the wok but that always seemed like wasted effort to me. The stock cube and the water would mix together in situ after all and my approach meant one less item for the washing-up bowl. I was not a fan of the washing up!

As well as the wok, I had a pan on the stove with some boiling water in it. Into this I dumped a handful of dry pasta before turning to look out of the window. It was freezing but Blake had insisted on going outside while I cooked. Obviously he couldn't stray too far from the house if he wanted to stay corporeal, although he had gotten a good way down the garden. Obviously my reach, or my bubble (I still couldn't decide on which was the right word for whatever it was) was quite sizable today. He was busy touching and feeling everything that he could. A number of my plants were getting mauled and I was grateful that, with it being winter, there were no delicate buds for Blake to crush. I couldn't help but smile at his obvious delight though.

"Join me," Blake suddenly demanded. He hadn't turned to look at me but somehow he'd known I was watching him. "Your thoughts gave you away," he answered my unspoken question. "Join me. Come! It's wonderful outside, the air is so fresh."

And that is how I found myself outside in the garden on a cold winter's evening in February dancing, yes dancing, with Blake. Unfortunately his idea of fresh was my idea of cold.

Blake was not the greatest of dancers. In his incorporeal state he was graceful and elegant but he'd spent so little time having to be aware of obstacles that as a real live boy he hadn't yet learned to pick his feet up properly. And my garden was not a nice level surface upon which to dance. I'd been promising myself for years that I would have my lawn levelled and re-turfed but I'd never gotten around to it. Evidentially my neglected lawn saw an opportunity to make me suffer for my shameful disinterest in it and went for the jugular. Both Blake and myself stumbled more than once.

It should have been a miserable experience but it wasn't, it was magical. Essentially it turned into more of a sway rather than an actual dance. Blake held me in his arms, occasionally turning me or dipping me down to the ground. Luckily neither of us fell! In time, he pulled me closer, cradling me gently against him. His bulk made me feel small, even though I definitely wasn't, and then eventually he kissed me. He reached up and with his forefinger used my chin as a lever to tilt my face so that he could lay the softest of kisses of my lips.

The world came to a complete and utter standstill in that moment. There was no-one else in existence, nothing else had meaning, nothing except for the feel of his lips on my own. I drowned in that kiss, but I also came alive in it.

"Wow," I exhaled when we parted.

Blake said nothing but a faint smile crossed his face. He tended to look stern but when he smiled his face softened. "Is dinner ready yet?" he asked, breaking the reverie into which I had fallen.

I was still laughing five minutes later when it was time to drain the pasta, which was then added to the wok along with some soft cheese and a little splash of milk. Et voila! Dinner was served. My only embellishment was to grate some cheese over the top before handing

Blake his bowl and a fork.

"I hope you like it," I said but I got no answer as Blake dug in.

Only when he was finished did he say anything. "That's the best dinner I've ever had."

"That's the only dinner you've ever had," I corrected, with a wry smile.

"True," Blake replied before lapsing into silence. It felt like he wanted to say something else but the silence continued unbroken. A weight settled between us, the joy and humour dissipated and I wondered what could possibly be on his mind, what he might want to say. I knew so little about this man, my soulmate, the Grim Reaper. And then I tried to stop wondering because I remembered that Blake was probably dialled into my thoughts. And then I wondered if I could turn the tables on him and hear his thoughts. Was that even possible? How would you go about reading someone else's mind? Or would I just develop that particular skill in time? I didn't have to try and read his emotions after all. It didn't seem fair though that he could already hear my thoughts but I had to rely on him speaking to me, albeit sometimes in the silence of my mind. I was considering the options when the phone rang.

I blushed, feeling like I'd just been caught with my hand in the cookie jar. "I'll just, erm, get that," I said as I stood. No-one ever rang my phone apart from my Dad. Everyone else I knew was a texter. Glancing at the screen I saw immediately that it was Ellie, not my Dad, and I knew something was wrong.

Ellie was in absolute pieces. "Em, it's Grammy," she sobbed down the phone.

"Ellie? Ellie, what's wrong? What's happened?" I asked. Anxiety and doubt settled into the pit of my stomach. The meal I'd just eaten turned to lead and I felt a wave of nausea wash over me.

"She's at... she's had a…" Ellie started to say before dissolving even further into hysteria.

I listened to her cry for a while before saying as gently as I could, "Ellie honey, why don't you text me? I'll be right over." I'd realised that there was absolutely no chance of me being able to ascertain what the problem was let alone where she was.

An image of Ellie rose unbidden in my mind's eye. She was usually the life and soul of any given situation. She was joy and laughter brought to life, a walking ray of sunshine. She always looked on the bright side. If Ellie was distraught, the situation was serious.

"Blake," I said, turning to look at him, disconnecting the phone without waiting for Ellie's reply. "I'm sorry, I need to go. It's Ellie, something's wrong."

"I know," he replied gravely, as my phone chirruped to let me know a text has been delivered.

Grammy's had a stroke. It's bad. She's been taken to the Vic. See you there? Xx

The anxiety and doubt from earlier turned into worry and fear. Grammy was 91, we all knew that our time with her was limited but somehow that didn't seem to matter. All that mattered was that she was most likely dying, we were losing her and it was so unfair.

I texted Ellie back. *I'm on my way. Xx*

"I'm sorry," I said again to Blake as I grabbed my car keys and some change. He made no attempt to move, simply inclining his head instead. I was out of the door before I had time to reflect on his words or rather his lack of anything to say. It was only later that I even thought about his odd behaviour.

The drive to Blackpool Victoria Hospital (also known as the Vic) passed in a blur. While Grammy was Ellie's maternal grandmother and not my own, me and Ellie had grown up together. Our families had always been close. Our mothers had been best friends since their school days. All of Ellie's grandparents had treated Scott and myself as if we were extensions of their family, an extra set of grandchildren if you will. Just like my grandparents had treated Ellie as one of their own. For us three children there had been no real distinction between the two families at that level. The three of us had grieved the loss of all of our grandparents and Grammy was the last.

Without really knowing how, I found myself turning into the road that looped around the back of the hospital to the big multi-storey carpark. I spotted my parents' car almost immediately as I circled the space searching for somewhere to abandon my car, taking comfort in the fact that my parents (and probably Scott) were close at hand.

The Vic, like most modern hospitals, is a collection of different buildings linked together by any number of corridors that all look the same. The only discernible difference between one area of the hospital and any other could be found in the bright and shiny main entrance, which was filled with shops and staff. In my haste that was all soon behind me, I quickly plunged into the world of more normal hospital paraphernalia. I felt lost within a few feet of leaving the main entrance and had to slow my pace right down in order to follow the signs for Accident and Emergency. If I hadn't done so I would have missed Blake disappearing down a corridor. I was so shocked at catching a glimpse of him that I came to a complete and utterly abrupt standstill. The person hurrying along behind me stood no chance and bumped into the back of me.

"I'm sorry," I said, turning to apologise.

It was a young teenager, evidently distraught. She had her hands pushed deep into the pockets of her jeans and the hood of her jumper pulled up over her head. She kept her face down but I could see enough to see that she'd been crying. Her eyes were tinged red and her cheeks were blotchy and mottled.

"S'okay," the teenager replied sidestepping me and continuing on her way.

The brief encounter slowed me down and when I turned back to where I'd last seen Blake he'd gone.

"Why is he here?" I muttered to myself before setting off towards A&E again. After walking for an eternity I became convinced of two things. Firstly, I was officially walking down the world's longest, straightest corridor. Secondly, I didn't just feel lost, I was lost. Stopping again I peered at all of the signs I could see up ahead. Nothing. Turning I looked at those behind me and eventually found one indicating a turning that I'd obviously missed. I backtracked and turned left, which took me outside into the cold night air. Not only was it cold, it had started raining and, in my haste, I hadn't bothered with a coat. I huddled into my jumper, comforted by the sight of another bright red sign emblazoned with the words 'Accident and Emergency' and an arrow. Once again, I set off in search of my family.

When I finally found the right waiting area after reassuring myself that I was going in the right direction by asking a porter who'd happened to cross my path, I found Frank, my Mum, my Dad and Scott waiting together in the entry way of A&E. My Dad was the first to envelope me in one of his infamous bear hugs.

"Where's Grammy?" I asked, "And Joanne and Ellie?"

"Joanne and Ellie are with Alice now. They're through there." My Mum indicated a set of double doors.

Without conscious thought I started walking. "Emma," my Mum called after me, "we're not all allowed in there."

"Let her go," my Dad answered. I could picture him putting an arm on my Mum's shoulder or taking her hand in his to stop her from stopping me. I didn't turn to look behind me though, instead I slipped through the double doors into what I assumed was triage.

Triage was split into a number of different cubicles, each of which could be curtained off for privacy. Some of them had been, some of them hadn't. All of them were full though. Nurses moved between the patients checking their charts, taking readings from the different machines, squeezing IV bags, making notes and handing out sick bowls. There was a relative amount of hustle and bustle going on but the place seemed well ordered. No-one stopped me though.

I didn't immediately see Grammy, Joanne or Ellie but at the far end of the room there was another set of double doors. They'd been propped open and through them I could see Blake. He stood next to a bed that was mostly hidden behind the door. I couldn't see the patient's face from where I stood but I knew who it was. Suddenly I understood Blake's earlier behaviour. I knew in my heart of hearts that he was here for Grammy.

"No!" I shouted, stepping in his direction so that I could see more of the room. Grammy was laid on her back propped up by numerous pillows. The covers had been pulled over her. She looked so small, so old and frail. From my new vantage point I still couldn't see Joanne or Ellie but I guessed they were tucked behind the door.

My bubble hadn't forced Blake to manifest but he looked like he always did to me. He was gorgeous and sexy, dressed all in black with a fitted jacket falling to his mid-thigh and his dark, shoulder-length hair curling loosely around his face. He glanced in my direction with his dark sultry eyes.

I stood rooted to the spot, unable to take another step and watched as Blake leaned over Grammy. He gently laid his lips on hers and breathed inward, lifting away from her, drawing with him a silvery substance. I watched as he continued breathing inward, righting himself until he stood proud, until her soul had been completely taken into himself. Grammy had passed.

Blake looked directly at me when he'd finished, when Grammy's soul had been taken from her body. His stare was challenging but also sad. He looked confused and, before I could move or make a sound, he disappeared.

CHAPTER 20 – BLAKE

Tuesday 12th February 2019 / Wednesday 13th February 2019

Blake stood on the roof of Blackpool Victoria Hospital staring absently at the town's iconic tower. It's colourful display of ever changing lights illuminated the night sky around it. The contrast between the towers halo of light and the unending darkness that had settled over the sea was nothing more than the natural result of day turning into night, but it was a stark one. Blake didn't appreciate it though. Rain fell in a constant drizzle and a chill breeze blew but he was unburdened by the weather. The resultant mist did not blind his vision nor dampen his clothing. The cold did not seep into his bones nor make him shiver. It hadn't even registered with him that the weather had changed since he'd danced in the garden with Emma a lifetime ago.

Blake was troubled by his most recent reaping. He'd known who Alice Elizabeth Edwards had been to Emma, he'd seen pictures of the old lady and had heard enough of Emma's stray thoughts to know that she was important to her. And so, for the first time in a long time, he'd decided to reap a soul himself rather than leaving it to a copy. He'd personally and consciously stepped in. Procedurally it had been no different to any other reaping. He'd executed the extraction without fault. He'd been born — or perhaps created — for the sole purpose of reaping souls, he'd come into being knowing how to do it. He'd never even had to think about it, whenever someone died he was with them wherever they were and whatever time it was, regardless of what else he was doing. He'd reaped hundreds of thousands of souls through the centuries. He'd reaped the rich, the poor, the young and the old. He'd witnessed every aspect of life lived by every single one of those souls, every kiss, every caress, every laugh, every betrayal and he hadn't ever come across anyone who'd known anything about him. But he hadn't always paid attention to the details, the lives of others had become insignificant to him. Maybe that had been a mistake, maybe he'd missed something. Blake couldn't think of any other explanation for what he'd just witnessed, but he didn't think he'd missed anything. He didn't have a choice in what he did and he couldn't just switch it off. Even when he was lost in thought he was also reaping the souls of the dying, he couldn't help but observe their passing. Surely if anyone had known anything about him he would have noticed, if someone had mentioned his name he would have been drawn into the reaping even if he hadn't been paying attention. Surely? But somehow he hadn't because Alice Elizabeth Edwards had known all about him and she'd been told about him by someone else, someone who's soul he assumed he'd reaped.

Alice Elizabeth Edwards had lived a long and happy life. She'd been born in the autumn of 1927 in Preston, she was the youngest of six and spoiled in the way that the youngest always is. Her childhood was remembered as one long summer, although in actuality the seasons changed as seasons do. On her twelfth birthday, the 1st September 1939, her childhood had come to an abrupt end, war was declared. Returning from a day at school, instead of the fun and games she'd expected, she'd found her family in shock. The mood was sombre and her parents talked in hushed tones; she sensed their anxiety but didn't really understand because she'd always been adored and cherished, she'd been kept an innocent. Despite her schooling she struggled to comprehend what war meant until her father and all four of her brothers signed up and left for the front. She stayed behind with her Mum and her sister and was told only to 'be brave'. Her home became solemn and quiet, her family afraid. She had to grow up, fast.

Preston was largely untouched by the war but families were torn apart, Alice's included. Her father and her oldest brother were killed in action, her youngest brother stood on a mine and lost both of his legs and the middle two came home when the war finally ended in 1945 traumatised by what they'd witnessed. In later life Alice came to the conclusion that they'd both suffered from undiagnosed post-traumatic stress disorder, they were never the same.

Despite the effects of the war though, despite the obvious impact it had on her family, Alice remained positive and upbeat. Somehow she managed to hang on to her childhood innocence even though she grew up overnight. She was full of life, the spoiled little child grew into a spoiled young adult eager for adventure. Where the war caused others to sink into depression, it served to remind Alice of the fragility of life. She lived every day as if it were her last.

And that was how she met Harold. It was May 1946 and the country was slowly recovering. Alice was 19 years old and loved music and dancing. She snuck out one night and went unchaperoned to a party. It was unheard of in that day but Alice didn't care. Within minutes she bumped into Harold, who exclaimed, "There you are my love!" as if they'd long since been acquainted. It was love at first sight and the two were later married on 1st September 1948, Alice's 21st birthday.

It was only after they were married, after they'd had two children together (Joanne being a later addition to the family) that Harold revealed he'd been keeping a secret. His family were the guardians of another very special family, a family that was uniquely related to the Keeper of Souls, the Grim Reaper.

Alice laughed at first, it sounded so ridiculous. It sounded like one of the stories she'd been told growing up. But Harold was persistent and eventually he persuaded her it was true. Alice felt hurt and betrayed because Harold had kept such things from her. Their relationship went through a number of difficult years, however it did survive and in the end it was stronger than it had ever been because Harold and Alice were able to be honest with each other in a way that few other couples are ever able to be.

Harold's story was that in the early part of the 11th Century the then Keeper of Souls had ripped his own soul from his body in order to give his lover a child. Without his sacrifice he could never impregnate her because his only gift was death. Only with his death could he give life. However, a human body could not absorb the entirety of the Keeper of Souls' soul, it was too potent, too strong. It split into two, with half of it being absorbed to create a child and half of it merging to form a new Keeper of Souls, one with no recollection of his previous existence.

The new Keeper of Souls was created fully capable of reaping souls, fully aware of the rules, but he lacked many of the original Keeper of Souls' abilities. In time, a guardian was sent to watch over him. And a guardian was sent for the child who grew up ignorant of her conception. It was a secret that her mother took to her grave. Only the guardians knew who carried the partial soul and what that child's potential was. Or so they believed.

As the sun rose over Blackpool Blake pondered what he'd learned. How was it possible that there had always been people out there who'd known about him? How had he missed that?

Blake had come into being knowing how to reap a soul. From the moment that he'd been created he'd been reaping souls, it took no conscious effort whatsoever for him. And whenever he reaped a soul he bore witness to the person's life. It was only a fleeting glimpse but he experienced everything in a moment. He'd gotten lost in stormy weather, literally freezing to death in colder countries. He'd dived into icy plunge pools, emerging from them shivering and blue. He'd dragged himself out of bed on a chilly winter's morning, hurrying to get dressed. He'd felt everything, seen everything and heard everything. How had he not overheard tales told of himself, how had he missed those whispered conversations?

And who was this guardian? Seith? Or some unseen entity? Why did he even need a guardian anyway? He was incorporeal, what could possibly cause him harm?

Blake stood lost in thought on the roof of Blackpool Victoria Hospital. He'd not moved for several hours but still he continued to reap those that died. As Blake watched the world awaken on one continent, on another he watched it settle and go to sleep. For some, the sleep would be permanent. In Anchorage, Alaska, he waited patiently by the bedside of a middle aged woman whose body was riddled with cancer. She had moments left to live but had come to terms with her impending death and was at peace waiting for her body to finally give up its fight. Elsewhere, across the Pacific Ocean in Tokyo, Japan, Blake stood in a small crowded house watching over an elderly gentleman who felt blessed even though he knew his time had come. All of his family had gathered to be with him and for that he was grateful.

Blake's consciousness was not with either the middle aged woman or the elderly gentleman but he was aware of them, and when their time came he would bear witness to their lives as he always did. Having learned to tune it out though had he missed something? He'd always thought it was like having the television on in the background while also having a conversation with someone in the room. Was that how talk of himself had gone unnoticed?

Absently Blake realised that the rain had eased. The storm clouds had cleared and the sun, as it rose above the horizon, had lit up the sky. Luminescent rays of brightly coloured reds, vivid purples and vibrant oranges had been cast from point-to-point.

"Seith," Blake spoke the word quietly, rousing himself.

The dog appeared by his side in an instant, one moment absent, the next present. As was always the case the air was undisturbed, no electrifying displays of materialisation have ever accompanied Seith's appearance.

"You were sent to be my guardian," Blake stated before lapsing into silence once more. His tone made it clear that he was not asking a question but that he expected answers.

"Why didn't you tell me?" he asked. And then after hearing Seith's reply he said softly, "That was not your decision to make. Did you know about Emma before I met her? And who is her guardian?" Blake asked before pausing to listen some more.

But before Seith could answer Blake felt Emma's anger wrapping around him like a shawl.

CHAPTER 21 – EMMA

Wednesday 13th February 2019

Grammy had died and it was Blake's fault. I'd watched him end her life, drawing her soul, her life essence, into himself. I'd witnessed him murdering her. It hadn't seemed real at the time but the more I thought about it, the more certain I became about what had happened. I'd seen him leaning over her and pulling the life from her body. Dimly, I recalled Blake saying that he was not responsible for anyone's death, that all he did was reap a person's soul. But I pushed that thought away, resolutely ignoring the small part of me that told me I was being childish. Anger had consumed me.

At the hospital I'd quashed the fury that had been building inside of me. Ellie had needed me and I had needed her back, so I'd kept a tight lid on my emotions while we'd clung to each other and cried. In time, we'd been separated and led back to the multi-story carpark. How I got from there back to my house (even though my parents had desperately tried to persuade me to stay with them) I'll never really know. The drive had passed in a blur with the auto-pilot option turned well and truly to 'on'. I saw the road but I didn't see the road. I saw the houses that I passed but I didn't absorb any of the detail, not that I really needed to, I'd driven between my house and the hospital on more than one occasion previously.

"Blake!" I muttered venomously to myself, pacing the length of my lounge, which was, let's be honest about this, all of four strides long.

I'd resisted calling for him the night before, focusing all of my energies on Cooper and Watson instead. They'd both been left outside in my hurry to get to the hospital and while I was so glad to have made it there in time, the consequence was that they'd been 'hedgehoged' in the rain, all because I hadn't thought to shout for them before leaving. I blamed that on Blake as well. If he hadn't been there, if we hadn't been messing around, I would have remembered to bring the boys in from outside before leaving the house. They always, well mostly, came on command and if I hadn't been in such a rush from the moment that I'd read Ellie's text I would have stopped for a second and shouted their names. Blake should have reminded me that they were outside, ergo it was Blake's fault that they got caught in the rain.

Each cat had been thoroughly towel dried and then he'd had some sweeties while I'd cooked, yes cooked, a fillet of fish for them. Despite the late hour when I'd gotten home I'd needed something to do to keep myself busy. I didn't often cook them their own fish but once in a while they deserved spoiling and I was very good at spoiling my fur babies. Ellie had approved when I'd texted her the news.

We were both in shock because Grammy had been taken so suddenly. It was so unfair! I'd only seen her the week before and she'd been fine. I mean, not entirely fine because there was no getting away from the fact that she'd had dementia, but there'd been no indication that a stroke was imminent. Blake must have known, he could have warned us, we could have stopped it from happening. He'd told me and Ellie that he could sense the impending demise of people. Why hadn't he mentioned that one of those people was Grammy? He'd said something about being drawn to death, something about being able to ascertain which choices resulted in the end of someone's life. What choice could Grammy possibly have made that had led to her having a stroke? It didn't make any sense!

After the boys had wolfed their supper, I'd snuggled in bed with the pair of them, determined not to dream about Blake. Of course by 'snuggled', I really meant that we'd all assumed our usual positions. Me in the foetal position on my side of the bed, Watson (ever the baby of the family) curled up in a ball with his nose tucked under his tail where my feet might have gone if it weren't for him, and Cooper, the giant panther wannabe, sprawled where Blake (or anyone else for that matter) might have slept if I had someone (anyone!) in my life.

And naturally, despite my best intentions, I'd dreamt about Blake. But it hadn't been the old dream, the one in which a tall, dark, handsome grim reaper extraordinaire stood in the corner of my bedroom while I willed him to kiss me. No, it hadn't been that dream. Instead I'd dreamt of him murdering all of those around me, sucking the life force out of all those I held dear. First of all it was Grammy. I relived what I'd witnessed at the hospital, saw again the silvery coloured substance being taken from her body. And then it was Joanne and Frank before my own family. Lastly it was Ellie. Time and time again I saw Blake take Ellie in his arms before placing his lips on hers for what started out as the most erotic kiss I'd ever seen, but ended with him drawing her soul out of her body. As he pulled away from the kiss a silvery blue thread of light was expelled from Ellie as she exhaled her last breath. Still standing, her hands flew to her face as it started crumbling into ash before her whole body simply disintegrated. Her eyes were always the last to go and with them she pleaded for her life, but Blake just laughed while he breathed in her soul. Or sometimes he smiled a chilling, cold, serpentine smile that made my blood turn to ice.

My dreams had grown increasingly disturbing until a little after 5am, in the pitch dark of night, I'd gotten up, showered and dressed. And then I'd cleaned the house. I wasn't normally obsessive about cleaning but by the time the sun had started to sneak over the horizon my house was spotless. Both my bed and the one in the spare bedroom had been stripped and remade with fresh bedding. A load of washing had been done and was on the airer to dry. The bathroom and the kitchen had been scrubbed, floors had been cleaned or hoovered, sides had been polished and then, when I'd finally run out of steam, I'd gone and stood in the bathroom and stared at my own reflection hoping to get some answers.

Having worked out that the strange faces I'd seen in the mirror previously were those people who'd lived with my soul before me, I'd sort of assumed that I'd be able to see any or all of them whenever I wanted to, that maybe I had control over them somehow. I had hoped that they'd be able to communicate with me, maybe tell me why the apparent love of my life would betray me in such a cruel way, but apparently that wasn't the case. Wishful thinking got me nothing other than a disparaging look at the dark black bags under my eyes and the blotchy looking skin that covered my cheeks. My usual, preferred look was less grief-stricken victim and more bright-eyed, bushy-tailed vet nurse.

When staring at myself became too much to bear because it wasn't a pretty sight, I'd stomped downstairs and started to pace, fuelling the fire that was my anger until it became a full-blown rage.

One of the things that I was apparently proficient in was the ability to hold an argument with someone else without them even being present. You might think that such a skill was a great thing to be able to master. You might think that with this particular talent I'd be able to work through whatever it was that had made me angry in the first place, so that when the time came for the real argument I could be rational about it. Sadly, you'd be wrong. Instead of calming myself down, I became enraged. I persuaded myself that my anger was justified because none of the answers I could come up with satisfied me.

And so I cursed Blake's name. He appeared immediately before me.

"Stop doing that," he commanded quietly, each word perfectly punctuated, his voice cold.

"I didn't do anything. I wasn't the one who killed Grammy," I replied as sarcastically as I could.

"Stop controlling me. I am not your puppet and I will not be treated in this way," Blake continued as if I had not spoken.

"How could you? Take her from us like that? Don't you care about anything? Anyone?" I asked, oblivious to Blake's demands.

"Who do you think you are?" Blake kept his voice quiet, his anger controlled.

"I mean, Grammy! Of all people." I, on the other hand, was getting louder and increasingly shrill. "Yes, she had dementia and yes, she was old and yes, she was going to die one day but I wasn't ready for her to go now. But you, you took her anyway. What sort of monster are you?"

"You do not have the right to dictate anything to me. You're nothing."

Some of what Blake was saying finally seeped into my consciousness. "Nothing am I? Well, if I'm nothing how come I'm the only one who can make you whole. Or had you forgotten that little titbit of information? Maybe you should have thought about that before ending Grammy's life because from now on I want nothing more to do with you. You can live out the rest of your miserable existence as a spirit, unable to do anything with anyone because I will not be stood by your side. Go on, get out and leave me alone!"

"Leave you alone?" Blake asked. "You can't tell me to leave you alone. Who do you think you are?"

"Who do I think I am? I think I'm the one who can control you. I'm the one who can make you do things. I'm the one who can give you a life worth living. And I'm the one telling you that you're a horrible, horrible psychopath! NOW. LEAVE. ME. ALONE!" I all but screamed the last sentence with no regard whatsoever for the neighbours.

"I will not. You cannot keep making demands of me and I did not kill Alice. It was her time, all I did was reap her soul." Blake's voice remained deadly quiet.

"Her time, indeed. She didn't want to go. She didn't want to leave us."

"Actually she was ready. She was looking forward to being reunited with Harold."

"Don't you dare speak Grandpa Harold's name!" I exclaimed, furious that Blake would suggest Grammy had wanted her life to be over.

"I'll say whatever I want to say about him. After all, I'm the one who's just witnessed his life with Alice. Through her I'm the one who saw him get married and have children. I'm the one who watched him get older. I'm the one who attended his funeral. And I'm the one who felt the depth of Alice's loss on that day. She wasn't just ready to die, she was praying for her death to come."

"How could you say such a thing?" I exclaimed. "Grammy would never pray for that! She loved us, she wanted to be with us." I spat the words before suddenly pausing because a stray thought from earlier on had surfaced. "You knew, didn't you?" I asked, turning to face Blake square on. "While we were sat eating dinner, you knew and you didn't say anything."

Blake didn't answer. He stood quietly, impassively, one eyebrow raised.

"GET! OUT!" I shouted, putting every ounce of mental compulsion that I could into that one statement, willing him to go, to leave me alone.

And with that, he was gone, blinking out of my lounge in much the same way as he'd blinked in. One minute he was there, the next he was not.

I dissolved into tears and let myself crumple to the floor, overcome with emotion, anger, pain, confusion and memories of Grammy. I tried pushing them away, not wanting to remember the good times we'd spent together, not wanting to remember the magical tales that she'd weaved for us. The tales of angels and demons and grim reapers. Wait! What? Grim reapers? I sat up, suddenly startled and brushed the tears away from my eyes before focusing on the wayward errant thought that had just occurred.

Grammy had talked about grim reapers. In fact, she'd talked confidently about grim reapers, as though she'd known something about them for a fact. Indeed, she'd had a way of making Ellie, Scott and myself feel as though we were being trusted with a great big secret, one that only she and a select few knew.

It had been years since Grammy had shared her stories with the three of us because as we'd all gotten older we'd had less and less time for the fantastical. I concentrated hard and flashed back to the last time that I could remember the three of us being enthralled. It had been winter, perhaps even approaching Christmas. The weather had been shockingly bad, rain had fallen in a deluge, and as a consequence, we'd been all but trapped inside. Scott and I had been taken with Ellie to spend the day with Grammy and Grandpa Harold while our four parents went shopping. Thinking back, they'd most likely gone out to get our Christmas presents, that being the day and age before internet shopping.

In the morning us girls had baked with Grammy while Scott and Grandpa Harold had worked together on something in his workshop. We'd all happily played together in our stereotypical roles blissfully unaware that we were falling into the gender trap.

It was in the afternoon that Grammy had started telling us stories, tall tales of golden coloured angels with feathered wings sprouting from their backs battling against horned devils with skin the colour of blood. As we sipped cocoa and munched on the fruits of mine and Ellie's labours, Grammy's sagas became more and more unbelievable until eventually she'd told us about a grim reaper, one who'd fallen in love with a human. No matter how hard I tried though, I couldn't remember any more than that. Had Grammy actually known something? Or had she simply been telling tall tales to keep three excitable children from getting bored?

CHAPTER 22 – EMMA

Thursday 14th February 2019

Grief had snaked its way around my heart and struck fast. For the last 48 hours the only persistent thought I'd had was of Grammy. She'd always been there for me and Ellie. She'd never treated me (or Scott for that matter) any differently just because I was not her biological grandchild and, as a consequence, I was as bereft as Ellie was at her passing. I'd spent most of the last two days with Ellie or on the phone to her. She was openly tearful, talking about Grammy at every possible opportunity.

As an alternative tactic I'd cloaked myself in anger. I blamed Blake for Grammy's death and I willingly fuelled that fire, constantly stoking it with any number of insults hurled silently into the ether. I still couldn't believe what he'd done. When I teared up, usually at the most inopportune moments, I wrapped myself in wrath, pulling it tight around me like a shroud. I focussed on trying to remember the stories that Grammy had told Ellie, Scott and myself. I'd even broached the subject with Ellie but she couldn't remember anything more than I could, although she did do a very funny impression of Grammy acting out her tales that had had us both laughing so hard that Joanne and Frank (whose house we were at) had come to investigate.

That is why on the way home after spending all afternoon and evening with our combined families, I hadn't even spotted the dark blue sedan (saloon) trailing along behind me.

No-one had been happy when I'd announced I was going home, so the fact that I made it out of Joanne and Frank's was something of a miracle. Or perhaps in hindsight it was actually a curse.

"Okay, that's me beat, I'm going to get off," I announced, extracting myself from the snuggle seat where me and Ellie had curled up together after being fed more food than was good for either of us.

"What? You're not seriously going home, are you?" My Dad was on his feet quicker than a jack-in-the-box.

"Of course I'm going home."

"It's not safe for you. Come home with me and your Mum," he implored. He'd used the exact same argument at the hospital on Tuesday night. It hadn't won me round then and it certainly wasn't going to win me round now.

"It was safe enough last night and the night before that. Anyway, I can't just leave Cooper and Watson alone," I shrugged off my Dad's concerns trying not to lose my temper. I knew he only worried about me because he cared but boy did he worry!

"You weren't driving home late at night last night."

"Nothing is going to happen to me on the drive home," I said, rolling my eyes.

"It might. You are being stalked by a nut job after all."

"By someone who is infatuated with me, not by someone who wants to kill me. I'll be fine."

"I'll come with you."

"Erm, no. You've been drinking." I busied myself gathering my coat and scarf from where they'd been discarded earlier.

"I'll come with you and sleep in the spare bed. You can drop me at home in the morning."

"No, Dad. I have work in the morning."

"You're welcome to stay here if you want to, Emma," Joanne interrupted, a faint smile lifting up the corners of her mouth.

"Of course," Frank quickly agreed with Joanne.

I turned to them both and smiled warmly. "I know. Thank-you, Joanne. But I just want to go home."

Frank grinned at me, despite his own grief. "You've always been Miss Independent, even when you were a little tot," he said. Both Joanne and Frank had witnessed the tension between me and my overprotective father many times in the past. As had my Mum. Ellie and Scott had always been so willing to do as they were told, to come when called, to go where they were told to go. I, on the other hand, always had somewhere else to be, somewhere else to go. There was a reason that I already had my own place.

"Ellie, do you want to come with me?" I asked, not giving my Dad a chance to argue any further although I could hear him debating the point with my Mum.

“Sand, are you okay with this?”

“Frank said it, Emma’s always been the independent one.”

“But what if something happens to her?”

“It’s her life Ian. We have to trust her to live it and to take care of it.”

While they bickered Ellie joined me. “I’d best stay. I’ll see you in the morning,” she said. I sensed that really she wanted to come but the obligation to remain with her Mum was too strong.

After that, it didn’t take all that long to extract myself from my loved ones but it was late when I left Joanne and Frank’s, there would be no play out time for Cooper and Watson when I got home. There had been hugs all round and at the very least I’d had to promise my Dad I would text as soon as I got home.

Joanne and Frank lived in a small village in Lancashire about ten miles away from where I lived. The village was really nothing more than a collection of houses and a couple of pubs. It wasn’t far from the motorway but it was tucked away from sight, hidden amidst the rolling British countryside.

The village could only be accessed by a couple of B-roads all of which I’d driven hundreds, if not thousands, of times. Not only did Ellie live at home with her folks still but my parents lived in the same general direction. I’ll admit that I wasn’t really paying attention as I drove. The magical tales that Grammy had woven lingered tantalisingly at the edge of my memory. I could remember snippets but not all of what she’d said. It was so frustrating!

“Come on, come on Emma. Think!” I ordered myself as I exited the village and plunged into total darkness. The British countryside at night, particularly in winter, was not renowned for being the most welcoming. The moon and the stars were all hidden behind dark foreboding clouds that scurried across the sky and rain poured from above. There was nothing to offer even the pretence of any light.

As I slowed to round a corner I carried on urging myself to remember something of Grammy’s stories. “Surely you can think of somet…” I started to say but suddenly, I found that I had no air left in my lungs.

My car had been shunted from behind. Despite my slower speed I’d been jerked forwards, held in place by my seatbelt. My feet slipped from the pedals and my hands fumbled with the steering wheel.

Glancing in the rear-view mirror I struggled to see what had hit me. Time slowed down as my car drifted towards the hedge. Was I going faster than I'd thought? Had I been hit or had I hit standing water and simply lost control of my car? It was a possibility. Or had I hit something? A branch? An animal?

I was trying to bring my car to a complete halt when it became obvious that I'd been hit by something rather than anything else. My car was shunted again.

Panic flared inside of me. Under the cover of darkness all I could make out in the rear-view mirror was a large, dark coloured car with its headlights off but I immediately knew what had happened. This was a targeted attack. I'd been so certain that I'd be okay but it looked as if my Dad had been right all along. My stalker was now making him or herself known. All the letters had suggested that I was a love interest, there had even been the suggestion of plans for Valentine's Day, for today. The letters hadn't read as if any of those plans involved me dying!

The second shunt had spun the back end of my car, pushing it (and me with it) further into the hedge. One of my car's wheels caught on the grassy verge and I came to an abrupt and complete halt. My seatbelt held me in place again but by the time the car had started to settle my head was spinning and my chest felt tight.

Before I knew what was happening, my car door was jerked open and I was being dragged from my car. Without any real thought, I glanced into the rear-view mirror again and saw my grandmother's face in place of my own.

Stay strong, she whispered inside of my head, communicating with me at last. She might have wanted to say more but I broke eye contact as I was manhandled by my attacker, a tall, portly gentleman with longer than average hair, hair that had already been plastered to his head by the rain.

He pulled me from the car and flung me to the ground all the while yelling. "H-how could you? How could you?"

My brains were still scrambled and it was all I could do to brace myself for the fall. I landed awkwardly on my right side.

My attacker loomed over me as I pulled myself up using my poor battered car for support.

"How could I what? Who are you?" I asked when I finally made it to my feet. My ankle shrieked in pain and did its best to cave under me but I gritted my teeth against the worst sensation of my life. I didn't have time to wonder what I'd done, it was all I could do to redistribute my weight in order to give me a soupçon of relief.

"Who am I? You mean you don't know. You d-don't remember

me!" my attacker exclaimed, a very slight stutter only just evident in his words. He gestured towards himself and I caught a glimpse of steel. A shiver ran down my spine. I had a feeling this was not going to end well.

"I don't know... maybe." I desperately searched my memory banks while calling for Blake. I'd been so angry with him for the last couple of days but it never occurred to me not to shout out his name. It was instinctual. *Blake!*

"How could you forget me my love?" He spoke softly, with a trace of sadness.

"My love?" I asked without thinking about the ramifications of my question.

"How could you?" he spat in my face. Obviously I'd said the wrong thing. He raised his arm above his head and it did not escape my notice that he was now holding the blade that I'd spotted earlier. It looked like a fairly standard kitchen knife, not that I had any idea how or even if that fact would help me.

Blake! I screamed in my head. "Wait!" I said out loud, shrinking back from my attacker as he shifted his weight, readying to strike with the knife. I found myself butted right up against my car. An image of Jessica and Fletcher hissing venomously rose in my mind's eye and I remembered who he was at last. "We've met previously. At Cedar's Veterinary Centre," I blurted.

"And? Before that?" his arm relaxed and the blade dropped away.

Before that? I thought. "I'm sorry, I don't remember meeting you before that. I must have bumped my head," I babbled, gesturing as though I'd hurt myself and taking the opportunity to wipe rain from my eyes. I was absolutely soaked.

"My love! Are you hurt?" my attacker asked with a degree of tenderness. It sounded as though he genuinely cared about me. "I never meant to hurt you. But you will cavort with other people. I had to punish you." The thing that frightened me the most was the fact that he sounded so rational.

"I don't know what you're talking about? I haven't been cavorting with anyone," I stuttered unsure how to handle the crazy person in front of me. *Blake!* I screamed again.

"I-I saw you dancing in the garden with him. They told me about him, they told me you would go off with him but I didn't believe them. I told them that you were mine. That we l-loved each other. That we'd n-never hurt each other. I refused them when they wanted me to work with them." While my attacker ranted he paced in front of me, the blade he carried gleamed wickedly in the light of my headlights.

Blake. Please help me, I begged silently. Surely he wouldn't abandon me despite my behaviour over the last couple of days. Yes, I'd been mean and spiteful but it had only been because I'd been grief stricken.

There's nothing I can do. I cannot intervene, he finally replied, sincere gravity in his voice.

Where are you? I sobbed. I couldn't see him but I was pinned against my car while my attacker continued to rant and I didn't dare take my eyes off him or the knife.

Behind you.

"Who are you talking to?" my attacker suddenly snapped. I don't know how he'd known but somehow he had. "There's no point praying. There's no God. And even if there were He wouldn't be able to help you now. You betrayed me. You betrayed our love. You will suffer the consequences."

"I didn't mean to. I'm sorry," I desperately hoped that if I could keep him talking I'd find a way out of this situation. Maybe if he told me why he thought we were in love I could let him down gently and walk away. "Tell me how we met. Remind me. You know, because the bump on my head has made me forget." My teeth were chattering with cold and fright now. The rain had eased an iota but I wasn't dressed for being outside. I'd anticipated a brief sprint from the house to the car, not a protracted conversation in the rain. All I'd put on over my jeans-jumper combo was a wind cheater and a scarf.

My attacker got a far-away look in his eyes. "How could you forget the night that you saved my life, even with a bump on the head? That was the start of it all. That was the night when I realised we were fated to be together."

Desperately I tried to remember saving his life but nothing came to mind. I'd never tried to save anyone's life, let alone his. I'd never been in a situation where I'd needed to save anyone's life. I knew first aid and I could give CPR but I'd never had the chance to practice my skills in a real-life situation, not that I had wanted such an opportunity. I'd never witnessed anyone having a heart attack or getting into any other kind of difficulty. I was fairly certain that would have been the kind of event that stuck with me.

My attacker continued, "We were at Francesca's. You were there with your work mates. Me too. And I would have choked to death if you hadn't bumped my arm."

The last time I'd been at Francesca's, a Michelin starred restaurant that Andrew favoured, was on the Christmas do. I remembered the evening all too well because it was the first time I'd ever seen Blake. He'd been standing in the corner of the restaurant and I'd been so intrigued that I'd gotten up to go and speak to him. I'd bumped someone's arm, apologised and when I'd looked back to where Blake had been he'd gone.

"I remember, I do. But I don't think I saved your life."

Actually you did. Blake commented. *I remember that night too although I hadn't realised it was you who'd saved him. He had such a rare probability that I watched: a 50:50 split.*

"You did. I was choking until you bumped my arm. You saved me," he answered smiling to himself before he spat, "but if I can't have you no-one will." He raised the knife and slashed it in my general direction.

I'd read somewhere that the best defence against a knife attack was to get as close to the attacker as possible and so I stepped forwards. My ankle threatened to give way underneath me but it was my ankle or my life. I pushed against my attacker. He was much bigger than me but I wasn't a weakling, I wasn't petite or slim like Ellie. I had some height and weight too. I pushed as hard as I could forcing my attacker to back off. He tripped on something and fell backwards.

Run! Blake barked. And I did. But I didn't get very far. I set off in the direction of the village running down the centre of the road, praying that I would meet someone — anyone — but my ankle gave way before I could get too far and I fell face forwards. The sharp pain of something cutting into my hands made me wince and my attacker was on me before I could scramble to my feet again. He grabbed the back of my coat and threw me over. My head smacked into the tarmac and a wave of dizziness washed over me. Idly it occurred to me that I'd faked a head injury only moments before and now I really had one. How very Peter and the Wolf. I almost laughed out loud but I was assaulted by a second wave of dizziness.

"How dare you?" I heard my attacker curse. Time slowed down once more and dimly I saw him raise the knife. I raised my hands to ward off the attack but felt nothing.

The last thing I saw before I blacked out was a real live wolf in my peripheral vision.

CHAPTER 23 – BLAKE

Thursday 14th February 2019

Blake had never felt so alone in all his life. He'd lived through the grief cycle on realising he was the only Keeper of Souls, the only incorporeal being in existence. He'd been in denial, he'd searched for someone, anyone like him. He'd had hope when Seith had found him, but his hopes had been crushed when he'd realised that he couldn't accept Seith's way of thinking. He'd been angry. No, he'd been furious, he'd screamed and shouted. He'd hurled obscenities at people that couldn't hear him until eventually his rage had settled into an icy calm. Eventually he'd accepted his fate and lost interest in the world around him. He'd fulfilled his obligations because he had no choice. He'd watched the goings on of the world because what else was there for him to do? Occasionally he'd been intrigued by certain events but in the main he'd lost his ability to care. He didn't care who lived or who died. He didn't care if people found joy or happiness. He didn't care if people lived out their lives in abject misery. And then he'd met Emma and a little spark of hope had been ignited inside of him.

Blake! Emma screamed. After two days of blaming him for reaping the soul of Alice Elizabeth Edwards she now wanted him. Blake resisted her call. He knew that if she commanded him to show himself he would have to go but he could resist a mere plea.

Blake had done a lot of thinking in the last two days but he was still confused. Things he thought to be fact had been proven wrong leaving him with so many questions. He had assumed Emma would help him find the answers but she had slammed that door shut. He met her hatred and aggression in kind. Her insults rolled off him like water off a duck's back. He'd had centuries of fuelling his own anger before lapsing into disinterest, hers was nothing in comparison.

Blake! Emma screamed again, her voice full of fear in his head. Blake felt it coiling around his abdomen, clawing at his throat, filling him with dread. He'd never felt such emotion in his life.

Blake! she screamed for a third time and this time he relocated of his own free will. He found himself standing in a field by a deserted country lane. An almost deserted country lane. Two souls burned brightly in the vicinity, one was the half of his soul that Emma carried, it gleamed golden in colour. The other was the more usual silver colour but it was darkened by an oily black and tinged with red.

From his vantage point Blake could see Emma pinned by someone much taller than she was against the back end of her car. Behind her car was a dark blue Honda CRV, its front end caved in. What looked like glass was scattered across the road.

Blake immediately sensed Emma's death. He concentrated on the possibilities and found only three. He watched each unfurl in his mind's eye.

Emma talked to her attacker, she kept him talking until another car approached. It was her father, anxious that she'd not texted when she'd got home, driving despite having had a drink. The approaching car spooked her attacker and he jabbed the knife into Emma's stomach. A sick feeling pooled inside Blake's own stomach as he watched his soulmate bleed out in the road.

Alternatively she ran. The most likely scenario was that she tripped giving her attacker time to catch her but there was a chance that she managed to escape by running.

Blake. Please help me, Emma begged.

Blake stilled. *There's nothing I can do. I cannot intervene,* he finally replied, speaking what he believed to be the truth. But was it? Never before had Blake questioned the fact that his only purpose was to reap souls. He'd never caused anyone's death but equally he'd never saved anyone from death. That was not what he was created for, he understood that intrinsically but was it that he couldn't intervene or that he shouldn't intervene?

Where are you? Emma asked. With her back to the car and her eyes glued on her attacker she could not see him standing in the field behind her.

Behind you, Blake answered absently focusing not on Emma but on who had her pinned. Blake's interest in people was so minimal that he didn't know everyone who had ever lived, or rather everyone who had ever died, but he did recognise Emma's attacker. As the Keeper of Souls he wasn't a walking encyclopaedia on who was who but he did have a good memory and once he'd watched someone he remembered them. He didn't necessarily know their name until after he'd collected their soul because that relied on him hearing it or seeing it written down but he did remember their faces.

While Emma was desperately trying to remember where she might have met her attacker previously, Blake was remembering the restaurant in which he'd nearly died. He listened to the conversation between Emma and her attacker.

"We were at Francesca's. You were there with your workmates. Me too. And I would have choked to death if you hadn't bumped my arm."

"I remember, I do. But I don't think I saved your life."

Actually you did, Blake commented. *I remember that night too although I didn't realise it was you who'd saved him. He had such a rare probability that I watched: a 50:50 split.*

Emma's attacker carried on talking before he raised the knife and slashed it her general direction. Blake didn't make any conscious decision to test his boundaries, he simply barked a command to Emma. *Run!*

Emma had already pushed out at her attacker and she obeyed Blake without any delay, setting off at pace back towards the village from which she'd come.

Seith, Blake called for his companion. The massive form of Seith appeared at his side, dark eyes gleaming despite the absence of any real light source. *Help her,* Blake commanded, pulling his scythe from the ether as he did so. If Emma's attacker thought a kitchen knife was a blade worth carrying Blake intended to show him what a real blade looked like. The curved scythe was the sharpest blade in all the world. Its point could be driven into diamond if necessary.

Seith had wasted no time, darting out of the field like a bullet, leaping it's hedge like it was nothing more than a minor inconvenience. Emma tripped and fell just as Seith's paws made contact with the tarmac. Seith didn't stop, launching at Emma's attacker just as he raised the knife. Seith's jaw clamped down on his arm, ripping his flesh open. Blood poured from his wounds but Seith was not finished. The beast pulled Emma's attacker from her and continued with its frenzied attack and then it was Blake's turn.

Unwilling to reap the soul of someone who had intended on ending Emma's life, Blake allowed the soul to rise up from the body before he swung the scythe. Cleaving the soul in two caused it to burst apart. Fragments of substance hung in the air before dissipating. All traces of the soul had been removed from existence.

Blake allowed himself a moment to experience the soul carriers memories before dropping to his knees at Emma's side. Tentatively he reached out and stroked her hair.

"Blake," she murmured. Her voice was slurred but Blake was content. The possibility of her death had passed.

"Help is on its way," Blake answered. Emma's father would not wait too much longer before he set out in search of his daughter.

CHAPTER 24 – EMMA

Tuesday 26th February 2019

"Blake?" I called, sitting bolt upright having woken in a cold sweat and found the rest of my bed empty.

"Downstairs," came his reply. My heart rate dropped from a galloping canter to a frenzied trot, slowing some more when I heard him on the stairwell. "Tea?" he asked.

"Yes please," I replied, dropping back into my pillows with a splat.

"I've made you one. And then you need to get up. Today is an important day and you haven't much time left to get ready."

"Urgh. What time is it?" I asked, unable to summon up the desire to move.

"07:44."

"Aww Blake," I whined. "My Dad isn't picking us up until 11am." Between my Dad, Ellie and Blake I'd not been left alone since my Dad had come across his worst nightmare. His words not mine. In the end I'd had to introduce him to Blake so that Blake and I could actually spend some time together.

"That only gives you three hours," Blake answered. He hadn't yet gotten used to how long it took us mere mortals to get ready. Of course it was easy for him. As long as he was outside of my bubble his look reset, and in the last week we'd learned that he could reset his look however he wanted. Much as I loved the all black look it wasn't very current and today he needed to look current. The nipped in, calf length jacket and knee-high boots screamed the 1800s and while that was still his preferred attire when he didn't need to fit in, today he needed to fit in.

Today was a big day for both of us. Grammy's funeral was scheduled for 1pm and Blake would be accompanying me. It was our first 'social' outing. We'd practiced keeping him in my bubble with family but today would be his first introduction to people outside of the immediate family. Not that we'd introduced Blake as the Keeper of Souls, only Ellie knew that fact. My parents, Scott, Joanne and Frank all thought that I'd just started seeing Blake before I'd been attacked.

Most of the cuts and bruises I'd sustained that day had now healed. Most of the physical ones anyway. The scarf I'd wound around my neck on leaving Joanne and Frank's had been shredded saving me from a number of severe cuts, any of which might have ended my life. My chin had been nicked and my stomach had a shallow slice on it but thankfully they were the only cuts I'd sustained from the knife wielding maniac. Other than that I'd suffered with a concussion, no doubt because of the massive egg on the back of my head thanks to the tarmac, my hands had had glass embedded in them and I'd fractured my ankle. My ankle was still a long way from healing but all in all I felt quite lucky.

"Do you need anything else?" Blake asked, putting the tea down and sitting on my bed.

"Yeah, about three more hours of sleep," I answered snarkily, not that Blake deserved my brand of wit. He'd been particularly attentive since saving my life. He was still the same old Blake, he still had issues of his own, some of which we'd started to talk through but now that he'd broken the rules for me he wasn't going to let anything else happen to me. As well as being generally disdainful and uncaring he was now also loving, towards me at least anyway.

"Tell me again what you saw when you reaped Peter Collins?" I asked.

"Cleaved."

"Whatever."

"There is a whole world of difference between a reaping and a cleaving," Blake answered. Apparently Mr. Particular was never going to leave us. "A reaped soul will be born again in time. A cleaved one will cease to exist. The spirits of those who are cleaved apart will never find peace. It is an action reserved only for the darkest of souls. I've told you this already."

"Yeah, yeah. Tell me again what you saw when you *cleaved* Peter Collins."

"I've told you this already too."

I wiggled about in bed, propping myself up so that I could glare at Blake.

"Fine," he muttered. "Peter became infatuated with you after you inadvertently saved his life at Francesca's. He was choking on a piece of food and when he reached for a drink you bumped into him dislodging the food. He became obsessed with the idea that it was fate that had brought you together, that you were destined to be with him and so he tracked you down on his computer."

"On social media," I absently corrected, having worked out that that was what Blake really meant during an earlier conversation. "Who knew that was even possible?" I asked rhetorically. Blake didn't fully understand computers.

From what I could tell from Blake's recanting of Peter's memories, Peter had used Francesca's social media presence as a springboard to finding me by using the pictures I'd been tagged in. By piecing together bits of information he'd learned where I lived and where I worked. And I barely used social media, it was a scary thought.

"Go on," I prompted.

"You know the rest. Peter started following you wherever you went and watching your house whenever you were at home. He discovered that if he loitered in the lane that runs behind your house he could watch over you undisturbed. He stalked you for weeks. At first he was happy just watching you but then he wanted more. He reached out to you with a bouquet of roses before writing you a couple of letters. His initial plan had been to knock on your door on Valentine's Day and declare his undying love for you. He expected you to embrace him and for you to spend the rest of your lives together. But then he saw us dancing in the garden. He was in the lane at the time. He then sent you a third letter."

"Which I only found later," I interrupted. Peter's third letter, which he'd delivered the day after Grammy had died, had been hidden underneath a random assortment of flyers and leaflets and put on one side when I'd scooped up the junk mail, planning to deal with it later. It had been full of rage and hate. Maybe if I'd read that before going to Joanne and Frank's I'd have been more cautious.

"And then he attacked you," Blake concluded.

I let Blake's words wash over me before answering with a pseudo question, "I still don't understand who he meant by 'they' when he was ranting at me."

"If they really existed."

Blake and I had discussed this point several times already. Peter had referred to a group of people who had warned him I would go off with a different 'him', presumably Blake. But Blake hadn't seen any memories in which Peter had met with a group of people. He had spoken on the telephone with someone about me and he had refused to do what was being asked of him but Blake didn't know if the conversation was real or imagined. Peter was clearly unhinged. Blake was inclined to believe that the conversation was imagined because he still believed no-one really knew of his existence, even though Grammy had known about him. I wasn't so sure.

"If they really existed," I mimicked, before flinging back the covers. "Okay, time to get up and get showered," I announced.

Showering was proving to be a bit of a challenge because my fractured ankle was still in a cast but nothing would have stopped me from looking my absolute best for Grammy's funeral.

I stood in the shower, hanging onto my newly installed grab bar with one hand, letting the scalding water wash over me while steam filled up the bathroom. So much had happened in the last few weeks. I'd nearly died. Grammy had died. I'd discovered my soulmate was the Keeper of Souls (aka the Grim Reaper). Sometimes I felt like the world needed to stop turning so I could get off for a minute and catch my breath. But that wasn't going to happen. Instead all I could do was focus on the task in hand and shampoo my hair.

It took nearly two hours but I was still ready long before my Dad was due, which proved to be a blessing because the phone rang just as I was hobbling down the stairs.

"Hello?" I asked when I picked it up.

"Emma? It's PC Danny Martin here."

"Oh, hi Danny." I'd spoken to the police quite a bit in the aftermath of my attack and you know what they say, familiarity breeds contempt. Or in this case a more casual relationship at least.

"Hi. How are you feeling?"

"I'm getting there, I think," I answered. "I'm still guarded 24/7 by my overprotective family though."

Danny laughed. He had now met my father! "I wanted to let you know that we're still searching for the dog that mauled Mr. Collins but we haven't found anything yet." Danny never referred to my attacker as anything other than Mr. Collins.

"Are you?" I asked. I couldn't exactly explain to Danny that 'the dog' had been Seith, the Grim Reaper's guardian, and that no-one would ever find anything because Seith was mostly incorporeal.

"Of course. It might have saved your life but it did kill Mr.

Collins. What if your Dad hadn't come along when he did? It might have turned on you next. We can't chance it."

"I guess," I answered lamely. What else could I say? "Do you need anything else from me or is the case officially closed, apart from the missing dog?" I asked, wanting to change the subject.

"I've got everything I need from you. The case is closed. We have both your statement and your Dad's statement on file now. You were damn lucky that that dog attacked when it did, you know?"

"Uh-huh." *Luck had nothing to do with it,* I thought but I couldn't exactly say that out loud.

"I don't often see luck like that in this job but the coroner did confirm that Mr. Collins died from blood loss caused by canine bites."

"Sooo... we're good?" I asked. The way Danny kept referring to how lucky I was made me suspicious about what he might be thinking.

After a long pause Danny finally answered, "We're good. The convoy analysis was quite damning as you know. If Peter hadn't attacked you when he did we would have been having quite the conversation with him about his behaviour. As it is, there's no-one for us to talk to."

"Great. So what happens now?" I asked.

"Now Emma, you get on with your life. And you live it to the full having survived what you did."

"Yes boss," I chuckled. "And thanks... you know... for everything," I finished more seriously.

"You're welcome Emma. Take care of yourself," Danny replied before disconnecting.

"That was odd," I remarked.

"What was odd?" Blake asked.

"Danny," I answered. "I don't think he believes that Peter Collins was killed by a dog."

"He wasn't."

"Well, not exactly but sort of and what other rational explanation is there?" I paused to replace the telephone handset on its cradle. "If Seith isn't a dog, what is it?"

"I don't know, just Seith. Definitely not an it though."

"Well, is Seith a he or a she?"

"I don't know that either."

"How was…" I paused debating whether to use he or she, "he I guess, able to do what he did?" I looked directly at Blake. "I thought he was like you but he hasn't got a me to force him to manifest. He shouldn't have been able to bite anyone let alone kill anyone."

Blake's eyes grew clouded and when he finally spoke his words were considered. "Seith is nothing like me. From what I can tell, Seith is what Seith wants to be when Seith wants to be. Seith has been my only companion for many, many years but I know very little about Seith."

Unable to think of a reply I fell silent. It might well have become awkward in time but no, we were saved by the bell. Also known as Ellie.

"Emma?" She called out before she was even through the door and in the house. "Blake?"

"Stood right here," I replied, having never made it much further than the phone point, conveniently located right by the front door.

I hugged Ellie, holding her tightly offering strength and support before she took a step back. "Hi Blake," she said, before offering me a sad smile, "you look nice."

"You do too," I gripped her hand in mine and squeezed tight. "You don't think my neon purple cast is too much, do you?" I took a step back and waggled my cast as if I were a catwalk model. It had been difficult planning an outfit for Grammy's funeral because so many of my clothes relied on me not having my leg in a cast. In the end I'd settled on some black leggings so that I could wear pumps on my feet, well one pump on the foot that wasn't half encased, and a long, dark grey chunky knit sweater over which I planned on wearing a black woollen coat with the obligatory scarf. In comparison to me Ellie looked radiant in a black fitted dress over which she too had a black woollen coat. She'd pulled her hair up off her face securing it into a French roll and had finished her look with a pair of killer high heels. If only I could still wear heels. Sadly they were too hard to manage with crutches. If Ellie hadn't been my best friend I might have felt jealous.

You look stunning too, Blake whispered in the depths of my mind.

You're biased methinks kind sir.

"Your Dad's waiting in the car. Are you ready?" Ellie unknowingly interrupted.

"I'm ready." And I was. I was ready to go to the funeral, ready to say goodbye to Grammy, ready to move on from being attacked, ready to face the rest of my life knowing my soulmate was the Grim Reaper. Whatever else life had to offer, I was ready. "Let me just get my coat on."

EPILOGUE

Tuesday 26th February 2019

"Well?"

"The police are continuing their search for the hound."

"I don't care about the police. The girl, is she healing?"

"She has a fractured ankle. It will take time to heal fully."

"But?"

"But she seems to be getting stronger and her control over the reaper will now start to grow."

"Good, good."

The End… or is it?

A FINAL WORD ON DEMENTIA

During the writing of this novel, I lost someone very important to me. My nan – my mum's mum – died on the 24th September 2018 having suffered with dementia in the latter part of her life.

Dementia is an awful illness that slowly erodes the memories and the personality of the afflicted. Thank-fully for us, my nan never forgot her family and we consider ourselves lucky because she got to meet both of her great grandchildren – Ewan and Esme.

However, in time she became unsafe living on her own. She forgot to eat. She had one too many sherries every day (having forgotten that she'd already had one earlier on in the day – sound familiar?). She forgot which house was her own. She became increasingly unsteady on her feet.

The hardest day of my life was the day that I took her into care, but the staff who looked after her were amazing. They made sure that she enjoyed her life even though she didn't know what day of the week it was. They baked with her. They sang songs with her. They watched movies with her. They made sure she was clean, albeit she often had on far too many clothes!

It was important to me that Grammy suffered with dementia. It might sound strange but I felt that by writing this disease into my novel I was paying tribute to my own nan, who also suffered.

For my own Grammy, Joan Irene Hibbard (1930-2018).

A FINAL WORD FROM THE AUTHOR

If you enjoyed A Grim Affair why don't you follow me on Instagram? I use Instagram to share my life as an author with my followers and to post updates about forthcoming events / publications. You'll get to meet Cooper and Watson, who are real by the way, and see where I do my writing as well as where I get my inspiration from.

My Instagram handle is: rachel21stanley

Printed in Poland
by Amazon Fulfillment
Poland Sp. z o.o., Wrocław

62077810R00106